Untouchable

Other Books Available from Geoff and Coy

Saul Imbierowicz Series
Unremarkable
Untouchable

Constable Inspector Lunaria Adventures
Wrath of the Fury Blade

ISBN: 978-1-932926-85-9 (paperback)
ISBN: 978-1-951122-00-3 (ebook)
LCCN: 2019945381
Copyright © 2019 by Geoff Habiger & Coy Kissee
Cover Photo: Carousel Horse Ride by Racheal Grazias, Shutterstock royalty-free stock photo ID: 24257200
Cover Design: Angella Cormier

Printed in the United States of America.

Any errors or typos in the book were put there on purpose. Can you find them all? Maybe you'll win a prize. Or maybe we're just outsourcing our copy editing.

Shadow Dragon Press
9 Mockingbird Hill Rd
Tijeras, New Mexico 87059
www.shadowdragonpress.com
info@shadowdragonpress.com

UNTOUCHABLE

By

Geoff Habiger
and
Coy Kissee

Shadow Dragon Press

Geoff dedicates this book to his son, Christopher, who constantly inspires and challenges him to be best father he can be.

"Unquestionably, it was going to be highly dangerous. Yet I felt it was quite natural to jump at the task. After all, if you don't like action and excitement, you don't go into police work. And, what the hell, I figured, nobody lives forever!"

~ Eliot Ness

Chapter 1

"Why am I always partnered with the unholy leech?" Agent Christian Wright asked, rhetorically, as we rode in the back of the truck. He fingered the small silver cross that he always wore around his neck.

I kept quiet and held on tightly as the truck made a sharp turn. Agent Wright was in yet another one of his moods and I was tired of always trying to please him. I hadn't chosen to be this... creature, and Wright had never understood that fact. In my previous life—before I had died and returned as one of the living dead—I had been Saul Imbierowicz, humble postal worker. I had led a simple life, filled with all sorts of unremarkable things: chatting with my neighbor, going to work, and having Sunday dinner with my family. That all changed when my now-deceased ex-girlfriend seduced me in order to get me to work for Al Capone, who had then murdered me on the Michigan Avenue bridge on a snowy February night. Ever since then, my life was anything but unremarkable.

Now my name is Stanley Kowalski and I'm an intrepid Treasury Agent. (And really, what kind of a name is Stan Kowalski? Eliot Ness—my boss—might as well have just called me John Smith. Kowalski is definitely the kind of name that a *goy* like Ness would come up with.) I work with Ness to enforce the Volstead Act and

1

to take down the criminals that continue to make and sell alcohol in Chicago. We are also working to get the goods—any kind of evidence—that can take down Al Capone. A lot of guys I know (*used to know?*) would have killed to work as a federal agent. *I had literally died to become one.*

"Why is that, Saul?" Christian continued ranting; his original question was apparently not rhetorical after all. He still insisted on calling me by my 'Christian' name, which was all sorts of funny since I was Jewish. He turned to stare at me from across the bed of the truck. Boxes of bootleg rum—which were actually bottles filled only with water—sat between us. "Do you think Ness is punishing me?" Agent Wright had originally worked for the Bureau of Investigations, but after Capone had killed his former partner, Ness had convinced him to transfer over to Treasury to work directly under Ness himself.

"If he is, then he's punishing both of us," I finally said, "since I have to listen to your whining about it all the time." I smiled, making sure to flash him some fang as I did so.

Christian recoiled and pulled out a larger cross from the inside of his overcoat. He brandished it toward me with a slightly quavering hand. "I am a minister of God's wish that the world will not be given over to monsters."

"Put that away," I said in irritation, rolling my eyes at him. "You know that doesn't work." He'd been trying to repel me with that cross since we'd been reunited after my death. "Besides, if a holy symbol was to have any sort of effect on me it would need to be the Star of David. I'm Jewish, remember?"

Agent Wright glumly returned the cross to the inside

of his overcoat. I couldn't be sure if he was glowering at me because I was one of the cursed undead, or because I was Jewish. *Maybe it's a little of both.*

"And I wish you'd stop misquoting Bram Stoker," I chided him. I had read *Dracula* several times in the past few months, hoping that it would help me understand more about being a vampire. It hadn't.

"I was not quoting Stoker. I was paraphrasing."

"Whatever." I steadied myself as the truck hit a pothole. It was just barely two months ago when I had been made into a vampire. Whenever I thought about it, I couldn't help but to also think about Moira, my ex-girlfriend. She'd been a vivacious redhead and I had fallen head-over-heels for her. We hadn't dated for very long before I learned that she was only using me in order to get free from Al Capone, but the time we had together—before I had learned she was a bloodsucking vampiress—had been wonderful. Of course, once I found out that she was just using me we had a... falling out. Okay, it was actually a huge fight in which she nearly killed me but I ended up putting a chair leg through her heart. Even though Moira had been the one who'd made me into the creature that I am today, she was gone, and she was no longer my problem. I focused my anger, and the blame for what I had become, on Al Capone. He was the one who was behind it all. Al Capone was not only Chicago's biggest gangster—a well-known fact—he was also the city's biggest vampire, which was something very few people knew.

"Ness should have killed you when he had the chance," Christian said. "He's a fool to think that you are anything more than a monster."

I wanted to leap across the truck bed and rip out

Christian's throat. He deserved it for being such an ass-hole to me over the past two months, but that would just have made his point for him and I wouldn't give him the satisfaction. Besides, my Mom raised me to be better than that.

"I didn't ask for this," I said instead, for what must have been the millionth time. "Do you think I wanted this? Do you even know what kind of pain I go through every day? Do you understand how hard it is to fight the temptations that I have? Do you even care about the fact that I can't visit my parents or my sister because I'm supposed to be dead? Every single day I have to fight the urge to go to them and tell them that I'm not dead."

"Technically, you *are* dead." Christian pushed forward, catching himself as the truck made another turn.

"My point is that you know absolutely nothing about what I'm going through, so maybe you could just cut me a little slack. Remember, I'm on your side. I want to catch Capone just as badly as you do."

"The enemy of my enemy is my ally."

"Think what you want if that makes you sleep better at night."

Christian just shrugged and leaned his head back against the side of the truck. I did the same thing, leaning back against the rough planks and staring up at the canvas that covered the truck bed. I was tired. I hadn't slept since I became a vampire. I hadn't slept *at all*. I tried to sleep, but when I closed my eyes nothing happened: I didn't dream, I didn't toss and turn, I didn't do anything. When I 'woke up' I'd feel like I hadn't even slept a wink. It got so bad that I had snuck into a mortuary to try sleeping in a coffin, hoping that at least that part of Stoker's story had been true. It hadn't helped one bit, and I ended up scaring the night custodian half to death. It's only when I drank blood—which, to date, has only been cow's blood—that I would feel somewhat refreshed and ready to go, almost like drinking a weak cup of joe. I was beginning to think that being a vampire just meant being tired all the time. Moira was the only other vampire I had really known, and she never seemed to be tired. *Maybe she hid it better or maybe she was just used to it.*

I have to admit that other parts of being a vampire are pretty nice. I'm stronger than I was when I was alive, and faster, too. Ness had made me do a bunch of physical fitness tests early on to see what I could do. I'd been able to lift the heaviest dumbbells with ease and I could outrun everybody at the track. Apparently I was incredibly fast, but I was quiet as well. *As quiet as the dead.*

Not only am I physically better, but my senses seem better, too. I can hear whispered conversations from across the office as though I was standing right next to the people who were talking. I can also tell that Christian had a hot dog for lunch. Not just that, but I knew that he'd slathered it with mustard, sauerkraut, and onions as well. *Okay, that last bit might have been just as easy to tell for somebody who wasn't a vampire.*

The truck slowed and finally came to a stop. The driver tapped on the back window. "Guess this is our stop," I remarked. Christian remained silent as we climbed out of the back of the truck.

It was early evening on a mild, late-April night. The truck was stopped in an alley between two warehouses. We were near the South Fork of the Chicago River and our objective for the evening—another warehouse—was one block up the street.

Christian and I walked to the front of the truck. Standing in the beams of its dim headlamps stood the other members of our team for tonight: Barney Cloonan, a broad-shouldered Irishman, Joseph Leeson, the truck driver, and Thomas Friel, who used to be a Pennsylvania state cop.

Another car—a beat up Model A with more rust than steel left on it—sat idling in front of the truck. Eliot Ness opened the rear door and stepped out, walking toward us. "Are we ready, gentlemen?" Ness asked.

Everybody nodded their heads in reply. Ness started to turn away, expecting everybody to follow his orders. "Is Capone going to be in there this time?" I asked.

Ness paused, and although I didn't see the look of irritation that must have crossed his face, I was sure it had been there. I'd seen it enough times in the past month since Ness had officially been put in charge of bringing down Capone for violating the Volstead Act. I didn't care about booze and Prohibition, or whether Capone was breaking the law—I wanted to get Capone because he was a *monster*. I had been pestering Ness daily about when we were just going to go *get* Capone.

Ness finally turned around and looked at me. "No, Kowalski. Capone is probably enjoying a comfortable evening at the Lexington."

"Then what's the point?" I persisted. I ignored the looks from the others. "Why do we even bother hitting these speakeasies and breweries? It doesn't do squat. Capone just laughs it off."

"You know why, you dumb Polack," groused Friel. "This is the best way to shut down Capone."

"We hit enough of his operations," added Cloonan, "and it'll add up. He'll start feelin' the pinch where it

"Meanwhile, he continues to run around Chicago as king of the city," I said.

"You know we can't take Capone on directly," Ness said calmly. We'd had this conversation before, and I was still in the dark about whether Ness meant that Capone, the gangster, would be able to bribe his way out of any attempt to arrest him for murder, racketeering, or any of the dozen other crimes we might stick on him, or if what Ness really meant was that Capone, the vampire, would just take us out without ever breaking a sweat. (Not that vampires actually sweat—another perk, I guess.) Besides, only Ness and Christian know exactly what Capone and I truly are. Ness had said that it was safer if the others in the task force didn't know. I wasn't sure if he meant that it was safer for them, or if he meant that it was safer for me.

"Yeah, yeah," I conceded. "I just don't like knowing that he's still free to be the monster that he is."

"Monster?" laughed Leeson. "Tell that to the kids he took to see the Cubs play the other day. He paid for the whole orphanage to go see the game. He even bought them peanuts and hot dogs."

"Just stick to the plan and let's hit this distillery," said Ness. "Are we clear?" He asked everybody, but he was looking directly at me.

"Yes," I said, reluctantly. The others had stayed quiet.

"Good." Ness turned back to the Model A and got in. The car pulled away. Leeson, Cloonan, and Friel all got back into the cab of the truck, which coughed to life with a belch of smoke. Leeson drove, and they followed after Ness.

"Let's go, Saul," Christian said as he headed down

the alley. "We need to hurry to get into position."

I jumped to the top of a stack of boxes, then to the roof of the warehouse. "Already ahead of you."

Chapter 2

I settled into position on top of a small warehouse that overlooked the building that Ness and the others would be raiding. The warehouse faced the street on my right, and the back, where the loading dock was, butted up against the river. An old wooden fence separated the two buildings and I had a clear view, from my perch, of a small door set in the side of the warehouse. A single light bulb shone over the side entrance, casting a dim glow over the area. It was as bright as daylight to me, thanks to my enhanced senses.

Ness had a snitch—somebody on the inside—who would signal the team when it was time to hit the building. This was a small operation, a distillery that turned out a couple of barrels of cheap rotgut whiskey a day. It was actually strange that it was in this area at all, since a lot of alcohol production was done in people's homes. They'd make up batches of bathtub gin or whiskey for the men who worked for people like Al Capone and Bugs Moran. Having their production spread around reduced the risk of attracting attention from the police or suffering a loss that a large raid might have cost them. But somebody had set up this small operation here, maybe hoping to get a larger piece of the pie, and risking Capone's wrath in the process.

Christian and I had been ordered to watch the side

door and stop anyone who fled out of it during the raid. I was here because of my gift to see in the dark. Christian was with me because nobody else knew what I was.

Looking down from the roof, I could see Christian standing at the corner of my building. He was fingering the cross around his neck again as he looked up and down the street. I felt sorry for Agent Wright. He'd been the nicer of the two agents that I met when they had been trying to locate Moira. Agent Truesdale had been a tough SOB, and I think that Agent Wright had felt a little sorry for me back then. That had been before Capone had shot him and killed Truesdale. That had been before I had become a vampire.

† † †

It had been about a week after my 'death' that Ness had taken me to see Christian. He'd just gotten out of the hospital himself and was resting at his apartment. Ness, wearing a light brown overcoat and a brown fedora, knocked on Christian's door while I stood to the side, just out of sight. Christian opened the door, a bandage still covering the left side of his head where Capone's bullet had grazed him.

"What can I do for you?" he asked.

Ness pulled out a leather billfold and showed Christian his badge and Treasury Department ID. "I'm Eliot Ness, with the Treasury Department. I'd like to talk to you about transferring from the Bureau over to Treasury. May we come inside to discuss it?" Ness stepped aside so that Christian could see me.

His eyes widened, and his face grew as pale as the bandage on his head. His right hand disappeared as he reached for something on the wall by his door, then quickly reappeared holding a large wooden cross. "Be gone, foul monster!" His voice was shrill as he took a step into the hall. "I am God's instrument and I banish you from this place!"

I stared at Christian for a moment. *He's definitely not the same guy who'd apologized to me for Agent Truesdale's behavior and left me thank you notes anymore.* He stepped toward me, thrusting the cross into my face. Annoyed, I grabbed for the cross, but Christian pulled it away.

"Stop that," I said. "It's annoying."

"Why didn't you flee from me? You should be cowering from the holy cross."

"Maybe it's because I'm Jewish." I shrugged.

Ness put an arm around his shoulders and guided Christian back into his apartment. I tried to follow but found that I wasn't able to pass through the doorway. It was as though a powerful hand was pushing against my chest. I vaguely recalled Al Capone asking me if he could be invited into my apartment on the one time that he had paid me a visit. *Ironically, he was the only one who had ever asked.*

"Agent Wright," I called, trying to sound as polite as I possibly could. "May I come in, please?"

Christian paused, looking like he would just flat-out refuse. If he could keep me out of his apartment in this way, I don't know that I would blame him. Ness gave him a light squeeze on his neck and said, "It's all right, Christian. Saul works for me."

"Fine," Christian said, with a resigned sigh. "You can come in."

As far as a friendly, welcoming greeting it wasn't much, but the pressure on my chest disappeared and

I was able to enter the apartment. I closed the door behind me and followed Ness and Christian into his small living room. The space was neatly decorated with a couch and a couple of armchairs. A Bible lay open on a small coffee table and there was a radio against one of the walls, currently tuned to a news broadcast on WGN. The walls had framed pictures of Christian and his family—I supposed—parents and brothers from the looks of them. There was also a framed picture of Jesus at the Last Supper with another cross above it and a photo of a young boy—Christian, I assumed—wearing an altar boy's vestment.

Christian turned the radio off and sat in one of the armchairs. Ness sat in the other chair and I chose to stand in the doorway. Christian stared at me.

"Agent Wright," Ness said, getting Christian's attention. "I hope that I can convince you to come and work for me."

Christian returned his gaze to me and rubbed his hand across the beard stubble on his chin. "Actually, I was thinking about retiring from government service altogether."

"I'm building a special group—a task force—to take down Al Capone." At the mention of Capone, Christian turned his gaze back to Ness. "President-elect Hoover has made taking Capone down a top priority for the government."

"Good. Capone and all these gangsters need to be taken care of."

"So, you'll come and work for me?" asked Ness.

Christian looked at me again. "Will I have to work with *it*?" He nodded his head toward me as he said the last word, scowling as he did.

"I'm right here, you know." I grumbled. "What happened to you? You were really nice to me last week."

"Last week I had a partner." Christian spat back. "And you were just a regular idiot, not the creature you've apparently become."

That gave me pause, as I hadn't realized how close he and Truesdale must have been. I started to apologize, but Ness glanced uncomfortably at me and then back to Christian before saying, "Yes, you'd be working alongside Saul."

"Then my answer is no. I appreciate your offer, but I'd like you to please leave now, and take that... *thing* with you."

"Agent Wright, please reconsider," Ness said. He wasn't pleading, as if he'd expected to be turned down the first time that he asked. "After the events of last week, I made some inquiries. It took some digging, and I had to promise a few favors to folks in the Bureau, but I managed to learn a few things." Ness sat back in the armchair and crossed one leg over the other, his ankle resting lightly across his knee.

"Back around the start of the Civil War, a special group was created within the United States government. It was started by Allan Pinkerton, but President Lincoln quickly brought it fully under governmental control. It was called the Night Watchers and, for a time, the group was run by the Secret Service before being transferred to the Bureau of Investigations."

Christian was looking toward Ness, but he slouched in his chair and was idly picking at some lint on the upholstery. I was fixated on Ness's story though, and I hoped he would continue, as everything he said had sounded far-fetched to me.

"The Night Watchers were tasked with protecting the United States of America from all of the things that go bump in the night: werewolves, zombies, vampires, and the like."

"Werewolves?" I blurted. "Zombies?" *Okay, yeah, I know, I'm a vampire, but still.* Ness ignored me, and Christian continued to slouch in his chair, clearly unimpressed.

"Of course, none of this is actually news to you," Ness continued, "since I know that you are already a member of the Night Watchers, Agent Wright. You and Agent Truesdale were ordered to investigate the possibility of vampires being in Chicago, especially among the gangs, and to take out any that you found. You'd only had one promising lead—Saul's former girlfriend—until you learned of something much more frightening." Ness paused, waiting for Christian to chime in.

Christian sat silently for a moment, chewing on his lower lip. Finally, he sighed and said, "We learned that Al Capone might be a vampire."

"Because of Saul," Ness said flatly, as a statement of fact.

Christian reluctantly nodded. "Yes, because of Saul."

"In case you didn't know, Capone is back in Florida right now. Nobody in Chicago knows that he was actually here then, or that he'd even left Florida at all in the past month. The Federal Prosecutor's office is trying to get Capone back here to give testimony for something, but Capone's doctors say that he's been laid up with an illness. Of course, you saw Capone last week on the Michigan Avenue bridge, when you had Saul confront him for you. You'd lured him there promising to give him some financial books."

"That was Truesdale's idea," Christian admitted, giving me an apologetic look. "He'd hoped that we could take Capone down with a silvered bullet while he was distracted by dealing with Saul."

"Really? You sure took your time taking that shot."

Christian glared at me. "We weren't even sure that it would work. Vampires can die, but they have to bleed out before their wounds can heal. A stake through the heart, cutting off the head, or a whole slew of bullets will do the trick, but we only had one surplus M-1 rifle. Silver works against werewolves and their ilk, so we had hoped that it might also work to slow down a vampire's healing ability."

"So I was your guinea pig to bait Capone?"

"Yes," Christian said, not at all embarrassed by the fact. *He'd do it again if he got the chance.*

Ness held up his hand to me. To Christian he said, "Capone *is* a vampire, and he's still out there. Please, I need you to help me take him down."

Christian rubbed his chin again and looked past Ness, clearly considering the request. If he said no, it wouldn't have mattered all that much to Ness. He would be able to find somebody else to put on his task force. It was at that moment that I realized that Christian was my only real link to my past. He was the only person— besides Ness—who knew who I was before I became a vampire. Ness had told me that I couldn't see my parents or my sister, that I couldn't go back to my job at the Post Office, and that I couldn't have any contact whatsoever with any of the people that I knew from before my death. To the world, Saul Imbierowicz was dead, so having any connection to my former life seemed important to me all of a sudden.

"Please, Christian," I began. He looked at me, jaw clenched, and eyes narrowed. "I may have become a monster, but I didn't ask for it. I'm just as scared and angry by what happened as you are, and I could use your help."

"Help? What help?"

"Who else but you knows anything about vampires and what they can do? Who else but you can make sure that I don't get out of control? Besides, I think you *want* to get Capone. Not just because he's a monster, but because of what he did to you and to Agent Truesdale. I want to get Capone just as badly. Help us stop him."

Ness and I both watched Christian expectantly. He pulled out a silver cross from a chain around his neck and thoughtfully rubbed it a couple of times, then looked up at Ness and sighed. "Fine, I'll join your task force." He turned to look at me. "But I still think that you are an abomination against God. I'd rather destroy you than work with you, but if it means getting Capone, then I'll do it." He pointed a finger at me. "Just remember—I'm not your friend. I don't want anything to do with you outside of work."

I was a bit taken aback, but if it meant that he would come on the team to work with us, I'd live. *Ha, funny.*

"Good," said Ness, standing up. He held out his hand to Christian. "I'm glad you've come on board."

† † †

Christian had been true to his word. Even after working together for over a month, he barely tolerated my presence and he never stuck around once we were done with work. On his good days he was polite enough, but most of the time I think he just wanted to put a stake through my heart. He told me once that he blamed Capone for Truesdale's death, but he blamed me for getting Truesdale and him into the mess in the first place.

"I'm only working with Ness to get Capone," he'd told me one day. "Once that's done, I will deal with you, too."

I hadn't known what to say to that, so I ignored the comment, thinking that, in time, Christian would come to see that I wasn't the monster that he thought I was.

And how's that working out for you? Dad's voice said in my head.

Dad, stop. Since my death, my inability to see my family had apparently affected me, as now their voices would come to me as though they were present and taking part in my new life. It occasionally got annoying, especially when Sarah would put her two cents in.

I heard the sound of a car coming and spun around to look down the road behind me. I could see the car turning onto the road that would take it past our target. I leaned over the edge of the roof and loudly whispered to Christian, "Car's coming."

He didn't acknowledge me, but he did step back from the road, hiding in the darkness of our building. I kept an eye on the car as it approached, hoping that it would turn off or stop at another building. It didn't. It was a Cadillac with green paint and it drove slowly past our building. I recognized it immediately. It was the exact same car that Capone had driven to meet me on the Michigan Avenue bridge on the night that he'd murdered me.

The car turned into the driveway of the warehouse that we were going to raid, stopping just past the side door. I felt myself rise up and bounce a couple of times on the balls of my feet, like a fighter getting ready to enter the ring. *Al Capone is really here*, was my first thought. *Now I can finally get that son of a bitch.*

When the car doors opened, two men got out, but neither one was Al Capone. I hesitated, disappointed, unsure of what to do next. The men walked to the side entrance and one of them turned to check the area before heading inside. I got a good look at his face and recognized Frank Nitti from the papers. Nitti was Capone's enforcer. *Shit.* The only reason I could think of for why Nitti would be here was that somehow Capone had gotten wind of our raid. *They're setting up a trap!*

I didn't hesitate any longer. I jumped off the roof and landed lightly on the sidewalk. Even jumping down twenty feet I made very little noise and I surprised Christian at the corner of the building. "It's Nitti," I said. "They're setting a trap for Ness. We need to stop them."

I headed for the warehouse without waiting for Christian. "Saul...I mean, Stan" he called as he hurried to catch up. "Those aren't our orders. We need to abort the raid."

"I thought you wanted to hurt Capone." I said. "Because if you do, this is our chance. Frank Nitti—one of Capone's top lieutenants—is inside an illegal distillery. If we can catch him here, we'll have him dead to rights. There's no way he'll be able to worm his way out of it. It'll be a direct link between Capone and bootlegging."

"We need to tell Ness," Christian persisted.

"We don't have time." I turned and headed to the side door, my feet making hardly any noise as I crossed the dirt and gravel. Christian sighed and followed, sounding like a plodding mule by contrast.

We walked up the steps and stopped by the side

door. Christian pulled his Colt from its holster and nodded. Just as I put my hand on the door handle, the sound of gunshots came from inside the building, loud enough that both of us had heard them.

I yanked the door open and rushed inside. The door opened into a large warehouse, with wooden boxes stacked in even rows. The smell of fresh blood filled the air, making my stomach growl, even though I had fed before we got into the truck. I heard sobbing and pleading coming from across the room. I ignored the pangs of hunger as I ran to the right, around some boxes and toward the other side of the building. Two more gunshots rang out as I turned the last corner and skidded to a stop.

Four men stood together in a small group: Nitti, the other man from the Cadillac, and two men in overalls. Nitti's arm was raised, a pistol in his hand, smoke slowly rising from the end of the barrel. Two bodies lay in growing pools of blood on the floor. The coppery smell caused me to salivate and, for some reason, I was reminded of the aroma of fresh baked bagels from Feldman's bakery. *I love those bagels. Loved. Whatever.*

Nitti turned to me with a sly grin. "So you're the one," he said. Footsteps sounded behind me.

"Put the gun down," I ordered, staring into Nitti's eyes. "You're under arrest." Another of the gifts that I had acquired after rising from the grave was the ability to get people to do something with just a few words and a special look. I finally understood how Moira had been able to get anything that she wanted without ever having to pay for any of it. Well, that, and being a drop-dead gorgeous dame didn't hurt.

Drop-dead. Ha.

Instead of complying, though, Nitti just laughed, and I stared at him with a look of dumb confusion on my face. In a single motion, he raised the pistol and fired.

Chapter 3

The gun roared, and I suddenly realized that it wasn't pointed at me. Nitti had been aiming at Christian as he'd come around the corner. Without hesitation, I jerked to my left and was immediately punched in the shoulder as the bullet crashed into me. *Huh, I'm faster than a bullet*, I thought. *Too bad being bulletproof isn't a vampire power.* I let out a yelp of pain. *That hurt!* I'd been shot by Capone and that had hurt like hell, but that was before I'd died. I hadn't expected it to still hurt so much now that I was already dead.

Normally people dive out of the way of bullets, nudnik, Sarah's voice taunted me.

Clearly, I'm no longer normal, I replied.

Were you ever?

Shut up.

That's no way to talk to your sister, Mom's voice scolded. *Apologize.*

Mom, I don't have time for this! I'm right in the middle of—

Mom interrupted, *You heard me. You apologize to your sister right now, or—*

I couldn't let Mom finish her threat, as Nitti fired two more shots. I shoved Christian to the floor, out of harm's way. One of the bullets grazed my arm and the other missed us both completely. Nitti and the others took the opportunity to flee and I gave chase, ignoring Christian's protests to stop.

I ran around the boxes at the end of the row and saw someone leveling a Tommy Gun toward me. Images of the gruesome scene from the St. Valentine's Day Massacre, and the memory of Capone telling me that he'd pulled off the murders in order to keep the vampires that he couldn't command from rampaging through the city, flashed through my mind. I realized that I really could still die again, only permanently this time. My feet tangled at the sudden realization and I fell, which ironically saved my life.

I heard a laugh, and I couldn't tell if it was a voice in my head or if it came from somebody in the warehouse. I fell to the floor behind a stack of boxes as a hail of bullets from the Tommy Gun flew over me. Splinters of wood fell around me as the bullets chewed into the boxes.

All at once the noise stopped, but my ears were still ringing from the gunfire. I couldn't tell if the shooter had fled or if he was just changing drums. After a moment with no new gunshots, I cautiously stood up, using what remained of the boxes as cover. I could now hear the sound of a car racing out of the driveway and the squeal of tires as they accelerated down the street. Nitti had gotten away. *Shit.*

I walked back to where Christian was standing over the two dead bodies. He raised his gun as I came around the corner, but even after seeing that it was me he still kept it leveled at me. "Whoa, I'm on your side, remember?"

"Could've fooled me," he growled. "You let them get away."

"Hey!" I yelled. "In case you didn't notice, I took a bullet for you!" I pointed to the wound in my shoulder. "Two of them, actually. I saved your life."

"Jesus Christ is the only one who has saved my life," Christian said, but he lowered the gun and holstered it.

Satisfied that I wouldn't get yet another bullet for my troubles, I walked up to Christian. The two workers were dead, and the smell of the blood was intoxicating. Saliva instantly filled my mouth, and the sound that came from my stomach was loud enough that even Christian could hear it.

Christian turned a wary eye on me. "You are *not* going to desecrate their bodies, leech."

I looked up from the blood and glared at Christian. "You know that I only feed on cow's blood." As I said it, I couldn't help but stare at the pools of blood that were still growing under the two bodies in front of me.

"So you say." He walked away from the bodies. My own blood was pounding in my head, a steady beat of excitement, and I felt my fangs lengthen. As I licked my lips, I could hear Moira's voice in my head, mocking me. *Don't be such a wet blanket, Saul.* The glistening pools of blood were almost hypnotic, and I had to force myself to turn away.

A clatter of noise from the front of the warehouse announced the arrival of Ness and the rest of our team as they rushed inside. I hadn't heard them drive up. My ears must still have been ringing from the submachine gun. They turned the corner, guns drawn, but stopped abruptly as they took in the scene.

"What the hell happened here?" asked Cloonan. Ness holstered his gun and walked over to examine the bodies.

"Sa...Stan here," Christian said, jerking a thumb at me, "decided to rush inside like a jackass when we saw two new men show up."

"Dumb Polack," groused Friel.

"Hey," I protested. "Christian was right behind me."

"As you blundered in and nearly got both of us killed," Christian responded.

Leeson stepped up and pointed to me. "Are you alright, Kowalski?"

I gestured to the wound on my arm. "It's just a scratch," I said.

"And what about that?" Leeson pointed to my shoulder.

I finally looked at it and saw a large, ragged hole in my coat and a lot of blood. But I could tell that my shoulder had begun healing itself from the bullet wound. "I guess I caught some splinters from a box." I looked up, specifically catching Leeson's eyes. "It's nothing. It looks worse than it is."

"Well, then, I guess it's nothing. It must look worse than it is," he echoed. He turned away to look at the mess around us without giving my wound another thought. *Ok, so apparently my power* does *still work. So what the hell happened with Nitti?*

I looked around at the rest of the warehouse. Tucked into a corner of the large room was a still, about six feet tall. It was made from copper and had a deep golden-red color to it. Copper tubes were coiled like springs and attached to the side of the still. A low fire was burning underneath and clear alcohol was slowly dripping out and being collected into a bucket. Previously used whiskey and bourbon bottles were lined up on a table, along with funnels, corks, and smaller bottles of iodine, which were used to add color to the liquid. The iodine certainly didn't add flavor to the bootleg liquor.

I walked over to Ness. "I saw Frank Nitti getting out of the car. I thought they were going to lay a trap for you. That's why I rushed in."

Ness turned and pointed to one of the bodies. "No, they were here to deal with a snitch. I think this whole place was a set-up to ferret out leaks in their organization." He looked up at me. "You should have stayed put."

"Why?" I asked "How was I to know that they were here to kill some snitches? I thought you were going to get killed in the raid."

"But you let one of Capone's men see you, and you let him get away," Ness said softly.

"So? We've hit a couple of Capone's other places. It's not like he doesn't know that we're after him."

"But," Ness said, whispering even more softly so that only I could hear him. "Now he knows that *you* are after him." Louder, so the others could hear, he said, "Yes, but now he knows that people in his organization are working with us. Had Nitti killed these two and we didn't hit the place, Capone might have thought that it was bad information. Now he'll change how he does things, which will make our jobs even harder."

I let my head hang. *I hadn't thought of that.*

"Great," said Friel. "Thanks for nothing, Kowalski."

Turning away, I walked toward the front of the warehouse. *I did the right thing*, I told myself. *Ness doesn't know if they would have just bumped off the snitches and left or set up an ambush to hit us, too. And Christian could be happier that I saved his life. Why the hell am I even doing this?* I kicked at the side of a box, and my foot went all the way through the wooden side.

I heard my father's voice clearly in my head. *You're doing this because you know none of those* yolds *can. You're the only one that can stop the* real *Capone.*

But we're not even going after Capone, I protested as I pulled my foot out of the box.

Oh, and now my son is an expert at law enforcement after just two months on the job? Dad mocked me. *You think you know more than the professionals who've been doing this for longer than you? Hmm?*

No—I started to say, but Dad cut me off.

Of course you don't. I didn't get to be supervisor by thinking that I was better than everybody else on my first day on the job. No. I watched, and I listened, and I learned, and I showed them that I could do the job.

It's not the same thing, I whined.

Feh! Dad dismissed my excuse. *Don't be such a* schmuck, *Saul. It* is *the same thing, and if I can see it, then you can, too.*

I slowly nodded my head. As usual, Dad was right, even if he wasn't here to gloat about it.

"Hey, how about you get off your ass and help us, Stan," said Cloonan.

I shook my head, clearing it up from my thoughts to see Cloonan standing behind me, jerking his thumb up. *Shit.* I turned away from the box that I'd abused and walked back to the group.

Cloonan put his hand on my injured shoulder. I winced reflexively, even though my shoulder had already mostly healed. "We all make mistakes," he confided. "The secret to doing well in this job is to not make the same mistake more than once." He gave me a pat on the shoulder, and I winced again.

I walked over to Christian. He was writing down a

list of the items that were on one of the tables in his steno pad. He looked up as I approached, but he didn't pull out his cross or point his gun at me, so I took that as a good sign. Mom had always taught me that if I was nice and polite, people would like me. Christian was my only connection to my old life, to who I really was, so I *needed* him to like me. "I'm sorry," I said. "If I'd not rushed in here like a *schmendrick* then we wouldn't have been shot at. I screwed up."

Christian looked at me with a blank expression for a moment, and then I saw his expression cloud over. "You're absolutely right—*you* screwed up. This isn't a game. If you keep acting this way, you'll get one or both of us killed. I guess I shouldn't expect a monster like you to think about anyone but themselves." He turned back to the items on the table.

My heart started to race, and I pursed my lips. I don't know why I expected Christian to be civil with me. He hadn't even acknowledged that I'd saved his life. It was clear that, to Christian, I was no better than Al Capone. I started to say something but bit back my words. Clenching my fists, I turned away to see if Ness had something for me to do, hopefully as far away from Christian as I could get.

Chapter 4

It was several hours later before we finally finished at the warehouse. Ness sent me to find a phone and call the morgue to come and pick up the two bodies. That had alerted not only the police, but a couple of news hawks who'd showed up trying to find out what had happened. Ness dealt with all of it in stride, explaining to the police and spinning things for the reporters in order to put a positive light on the Treasury Department and giving credit to the police (even though they had nothing to do with the events of the evening).

The guys from the morgue took care of the bodies. After some photos of the still and the blood-stained floor, the two reporters had left as well. Ness told us all to head home and to meet back at our office in the morning.

I walked to the nearest L station and took the train to the Loop where I got off at the State/Lake station. From there, it was a short walk up North State Street, past the Chicago Theater, and into the alley that ran behind my building. Ness had set me up in this apartment, and nobody else knew that I lived here. After all of the encounters that I had with Mrs. Rabinowitz at my old apartment, I had been much more careful about how I came and went.

In the old days—the simple days before I had died—

my apartment had been on the top floor of an old tenement along North Racine. Mrs. Rabinowitz had been my nosy neighbor who kept a close eye on me. She'd been spying on me for my mother, keeping Mom informed about my love life (or lack thereof) and anything else that was going on. She would also deliver terse messages from my mother—usually telling me to get something from Feldman's or to remind me to attend Temple—while she chided me about something else. I was always polite with Mrs. R., but only because Mom had raised me that way. It had been impossible to keep any secrets from Mrs. R., so I wanted to avoid any similarly nosy neighbors at my new apartment, not just for my privacy, but for their protection, after Mrs. R. had been brutally murdered. I had taken to using the fire escape to reach the roof, so that I could take the stairs down from there to my top floor apartment without being seen by any of my neighbors.

Tonight—well, this morning, since it was past midnight—I felt drained as I climbed the fire escape to the roof. I had eaten dinner with the other members of the team before the raid, but I'd only fed on a little blood that I had kept in a Thermos before getting into the truck. Eating real food allowed me to fit in, and the food didn't taste any different as far as I could tell, but apparently it didn't do anything to curb my hunger. I could stuff my face, but if I hadn't fed on any blood, I'd still have a gnawing hunger in the pit of my stomach after the meal, the same way that I felt tonight after seeing those two bodies. Right now, I was so tired that the only thing I wanted to do was go home so that I could pour myself a big glass of cow's blood and lay down to rest for a while. I had given up on ever sleeping again.

The door on the roof that accessed the stairs opened quietly. I had taken the liberty of making sure that the hinges were all well-oiled. I didn't want any of my neighbors to wonder why somebody was using the stairs to the roof at all hours of the night. I headed downstairs and turned down the hall toward my apartment. The small piece of paper that I'd put between the door and the jamb was still there, so I knew that I'd not had any uninvited visitors (a trick that Ness had taught me). My last apartment had felt like a turnstile at Wrigley Field on game day, with so many people coming and going as they pleased. I'd also added a second lock, belatedly following the advice that the late Mrs. R. had given me about my previous place.

As I stood in front of the door, about to put my key in the first lock, the hairs on the back of my neck stood up on end. This was immediately followed by a tickling sensation running down my spine, like a hundred ants had all decided to go for a walk from my neck down my back. It was like the saying, that somebody had just walked across my grave. *That would be quite a feat*, I thought, *since my grave was empty and I was a walking dead man.*

I'd had similar sensations on a couple of prior occasions when we'd been on stakeouts for Capone's gang. We'd always been watching the places from a distance and we'd see gang members entering buildings. One time we'd even seen Capone, but we hadn't been in a position to do anything about it. On those occasions, it had just been a quick tickle that had immediately come and gone. I had thought that it had been nerves, maybe from my being inexperienced at this new job, and at the thought that, even though Capone had been so close, I was powerless to do anything about it. But now it was a strong feeling and I somehow knew, instinctively—deep in my gut—that another vampire was nearby.

I looked to my left and right. "Who's there?" I called out. There were some dim light bulbs in the hallway, but to me they shone brightly, and I could clearly see that there was nobody in the hallway with me. The tingling sensation wouldn't go away, though.

Then, the door from my neighbor's apartment that was right across the hall from mine opened. I turned around hesitantly, my reflexes and senses deadened from my hunger and exhaustion. A figure stood in the doorway, silhouetted by a light from within the apartment.

"Mr. Imbierowicz," said a voice that I instantly recognized. "You are a difficult man to locate." I sucked in a breath that I didn't need and I stopped moving, as if a stiff winter wind off Lake Michigan had frozen me in place.

The figure stepped back and gestured for me to enter the apartment. I could now clearly see Al Capone's leering face in the light. "Please come in," Capone invited. "We have much to discuss, you and I."

Chapter 5

My throat had immediately gone dry—as parched as the Sahara Desert—as soon as I recognized Capone's voice. He stood in my neighbor's—Mr. Stafford's—doorway. Capone wore a tailored, robin's egg blue suit, with a matching vest and a starched snow-white shirt. A bright, scarlet-colored silk tie was knotted at his neck. He stood there, holding the door open and gesturing for me to enter.

I swallowed a couple of times and tried to wet my lips, but my mouth had gone just as dry as my throat. Sure, I wanted to get Capone, to make him pay for what he'd done to me. I'd been bragging to Ness and Christian for months about just how I was going to make Al Capone pay. Now, with him barely five feet away, I was rooted in place, unable to react. *It's got to be the fatigue*, I told myself. *Or maybe it's the shock*. I had certainly not planned on my next encounter with Al Capone being in my neighbor's apartment.

I finally got enough spit to unstick my lips and said, "What... what do you want?" Not exactly a heroic opening line, but I was working hard just to keep my knees from knocking together.

"Tsk, tsk. I thought Mrs. Imbierowicz raised you better than that."

"She raised me to be polite to people, even to total

strangers. But not to monsters like you."

Capone gave me a sardonic grin. "It seems that in addition to being rude, you've grown a pair of balls since our last meeting."

"I guess that getting murdered can have that effect on a person," I said, looking Capone directly in his eyes. That was apparently a mistake.

"Come here, Mr. Imbierowicz," Capone commanded.

The words were like a physical force, compelling me to do as Capone had ordered. It was different from the time that Moira took me to meet Capone at his home and he'd ordered me to steal some books from the Feds. I'd been pretty mad at the time, what with being pulled in so many different directions and being threatened by Bugs Moran and Agents Truesdale and Wright. Having Capone trying to order me to do something had made me snap—probably foolishly—and I'd told Capone no. He became so enraged at my refusal that I was sure that he was going to attack me right there in his office. Instead, he'd turned his anger on Moira and had left me alone. *If I was unaffected by Capone's command then*, I asked myself in a panic, *why can he affect me now*?

My right foot had already taken one step toward Capone, as if I was a puppet and somebody else was moving my leg. I felt the same thing happening to my left foot and I was powerless to resist. I tried to will my feet to stop moving, to remain standing by my door, but I was inevitably pulled toward Mr. Stafford's apartment. It gave me an unsettled feeling as I had used this same trick on other people. Getting a complete stranger to do what you wanted them to had been a useful skill, but now my stomach churned as I realized just what it felt like to have absolutely no way to prevent yourself from doing something that was completely against your will. *Was this what Moira had felt when Capone had ordered her to kill me?*

Capone stepped aside as I entered the apartment and he closed the door behind me. The urge to do Capone's bidding was gone now that I had complied. "Please have a seat, Mr. Imbierowicz." Capone gestured to a chair in Mr. Stafford's living room.

I should have left, just opened the door and ran, but now that I was caught, I was curious as to what Capone wanted. I also wasn't sure if I could leave, even though I felt like I was free of Capone's compulsion. *Could he still order me to stay?* He'd just proved that I couldn't resist his power.

Capone must have thought that I was hesitating to take the seat out of fear. *He wasn't entirely wrong.* "Please, Mr. Imbierowicz," he took a seat on Mr. Stafford's couch. "I merely want to have words with you." His voice was silky smooth and there was no feeling of coercion behind it this time.

I finally sat down in the armchair, idly looking around Mr. Stafford's apartment. It was identical to mine in layout, although his was better decorated. He was a middle-aged bachelor who worked as a salesman for a bank or something. *Maybe an insurance company?* I'd only met the man once and hadn't bothered to really learn anything about him. I had wanted to keep as much distance from my neighbors as I could.

"What have you done with Mr. Stafford?" I asked.

"Mr. Stafford is with one of my associates," Capone replied. "He is completely unharmed, for the moment, anyway."

"If you hurt him..."

Capone laughed softly. "Why would I want to harm your neighbor when all I want to do is to talk to you?" He gave me a curious look with his grey eyes.

"Why even meet here at all then?" I tried to ignore Capone's look, not wanting to meet his gaze again. I focused on a picture that hung on the wall behind him. It was a painting of a nondescript wooded glade.

"Would you have invited me into your apartment?"

I shook my head.

"This is not the kind of talk we could have down at the corner diner over coffee and donuts." Capone chuckled softly to himself, apparently at the humor of him ever deigning to eat anything in a diner. "Mr. Imbierowicz, what do you know about my kind?" he asked.

"You mean gangsters?" My head was swimming in a fog and I wasn't thinking straight. I wished that I had at least had the opportunity to feed again so that I could meet Capone on equal footing. Capone gave another small chuckle, a polite laugh that an adult might give a child for asking a silly question.

You putz, *he means vampires,* Sarah said.

Oh, right.

"I'm not here to talk to you about gangs. I'm a responsible citizen of the community and I have no knowledge of any sort of criminal activities." He gave me a knowing smile to go along with the lie. "No, Mr. Imbierowicz, I'm talking about my race. An ancient and proud race, that you now have the fortune to be a member of."

"Vampires," I said.

Capone grimaced at the word but bowed his head to acknowledge it. "It's such a crude term, but yes. We have been a part of this world for as long as man has, and while we all start out being born as men and women, to become one of us is to evolve beyond being merely human. God has bestowed upon us gifts that give us power over man, and we must use that power to sustain ourselves, lest we become as extinct as the dodo or the passenger pigeon."

Capone sounded like a Sunday preacher—or a Saturday rabbi—and it seemed odd coming from him. It didn't fit with any of the images I had of Capone, but something about his statement nagged at me.

"If vampires are so powerful, then why aren't you running the whole country?"

"Who says we aren't?" Capone replied, a slight gleam in his eye.

I considered this and thought that he was just trying to scare me. "If that was true, people would know," I said, but it sounded lame even as the words left my mouth. *Would we know, though?*

Capone shook his head, as if I was a child who didn't understand the real world. *Maybe I am.*

"Throughout history some of us have risen to power, but regular people are scared sheep, and they lash out unpredictably. There was a Romanian Prince who lived centuries ago called Vlad Dragulya. He was one of us. Historians call him Vlad Tepes, or Vlad the Impaler, because they want to paint him as a monster. His people revolted against his rule and ended up cutting off his head." Capone drew a finger across his neck. "Vlad is said to have been Bram Stoker's inspiration for the character in that abominable novel of his."

I'd been reading *Dracula* a lot, hoping to learn more about what a vampire was supposed to be. It's not really the best source material. *Hell, it's not like the Chicago Public Library has any other books on being a vampire.*

"So, Dracula isn't a real vampire?"

Capone gave a full-throated laugh. "Dracula is a figment from Stoker's imagination. He is solely a work of fiction and is pure drivel. Surely you know that, Mr. Imbierowicz. Are you repelled by the cross? Do you sleep in a coffin?"

I had to admit that Capone was right about that. "But some of it's right," I countered, ticking off on my fingers. "The need to drink blood. The power to command others."

"Stoker got lucky on a few things," Capone allowed. "We've lived as myth and legend in the human psyche for millennia, so he was bound to get a few things right." Capone gave me a broad smile and held out his hands. "But you are a virgin in our ways and our customs."

Capone was right, I had so many questions. *But do I dare ask Capone?*

And what, Dad said. *You know of any other vampires that you can ask?*

No. The only vampires I knew of were Mr. Brown (who'd tried to strangle me at the garage where the St. Valentine's Day Massacre had occurred), Moira (who was dead), and Al Capone.

Capone looked at me with a patient, almost paternal expression. "I do have a lot of questions," I admitted. "I know I am stronger and faster than people, and that my injuries heal quickly. I've even been able to command some people to do what I want them to do."

Capone nodded sagely, waiting for me to continue. "But there are so many things that I don't know. Do I have any other abilities? Can I turn into a bat or command wolves and other creatures? Why can't I sleep? Why do I feel so tired all the time?"

Capone gave me a fatherly laugh. "It's understand-able that you have these questions. All of the Reborn are just like you. Confused, unsure of what they are now. You want answers. I can provide them to you."

Finally, some answers, I thought. But Dad's voice practically yelled at me. *You wanted to kill him before, for making you into this monster. Now you want to be his chum? Stop being a* schmuck!

Dad was right. *Capone is the one who's responsible for me being a vampire, and he's Chicago's biggest gang-ster. How can I possibly trust him? Why should I listen to anything he says? He's nothing more than a monster, like me.*

"Look, Saul," Capone said, and I glanced at his face for a brief moment, surprised. *He's never used my first name before.* "I understand what you are going through. You think I'm a monster, and who can blame you? All you've had are Stoker's fiction and your idiotic co-work-ers to guide you."

"And you'll just answer my questions?" I couldn't keep the incredulity from my voice. "What's the catch? The last time you wanted something from me you threatened my family."

Capone ran a hand down his tie, smoothing it. "That's all in the past," he said. "Your folks think that you are dead, so I have no reason to threaten you, or them."

I didn't buy it. He had to know that I still cared about my family, but if he wasn't going to make a threat against them I certainly wasn't going to complain. "So, instead you'll threaten my co-workers?"

"Your co-workers don't scare me and killing them would bring too much attention to their pitiful attempts to pin every crime in Chicago on me. Your boss, Eliot

Ness, will become frustrated when he realizes that he just can't catch me at anything and he'll be reassigned as a failure."

Again, I didn't believe him, but he wasn't making wild threats like he'd done prior to my death. *Can I actually trust him?*

Capone stood up from the couch and moved toward the short hall that I knew led to Mr. Stafford's bedroom. "Let me demonstrate for you my good intentions, Mr. Imbierowicz. I will answer one of your questions for you." He turned back to face me. "The reason for your fatigue is that you've not fed."

Not fed? Does he think I'm narish? "I'm not stupid," I said, even though I did sound a bit stupid just for saying it. "I fed earlier today."

"Let me guess—cow's blood." Capone made it a statement. "I know it wasn't human blood, because you said you're tired all the time. I also assume that you are still clinging to the misguided notions of your religion and therefore won't drink pig's blood."

"So," I drew out the word, trying to think about his statement. "If I drink pig's blood, I won't be tired?" *If violating the rules on kosher food meant that I wouldn't be tired anymore, I might just have to try it.*

"No." My shoulders sagged at the single word. "Feeding on animal blood will keep us from starving to death, but it's a poor substitute. The only way that you won't feel fatigued is to feed on human blood. It has sustained our race throughout history. Without it, we are not at our full potential." He turned and called up the hallway. "Mr. Nitti! Now, if you please."

I was surprised as the bedroom door opened and Frank Nitti came down the hall, leading along my neighbor, Mr. Stafford. I stood up from the chair and took a step toward them. I had thought that we were alone in the apartment when Capone said that Mr. Stafford was with his associates. My neighbor looked pale and ashen, his eyes wide as he looked from me to Capone. He wore a long nightshirt and padded along in stocking feet. Nitti handed Mr. Stafford off to Capone, who gently took hold of his arm. Nitti walked over to take a seat on the couch, giving me a sneer as he passed.

Mr. Stafford was visibly shaking. I could see his hands trembling as he stood next to Capone. His eyes were wide and the look on his face reminded me of the look on the faces of the cattle at the stockyards. I clenched my hands together into tight fists. I had never wanted my neighbors to get caught up in what I had become, and I felt powerless right now to do anything for Mr. Stafford.

"To truly become one of the Enlightened," Capone said, "You must feed properly."

Before I could react, Capone tilted his head, long fangs jutting from his mouth. I started to say something, to scream for Capone to stop, but the words had no chance to escape my lips before he bit deeply into Mr. Stafford's neck.

Chapter 6

I stood frozen in shock as blood—a deep crimson color—welled around Capone's fat lips. I was surprised by how little blood was lost. There was no great gout of blood like I'd imagined there would be. In fact, there was just a small trail of blood that traced a short red line down Mr. Stafford's neck. There wasn't even a single drop of blood on the collar of his nightshirt.

Mr. Stafford's eyes were wide, his pupils narrowed to tiny points, and I saw him try to grab at Capone with his free arm, but Capone must have had an iron grip on his left arm that kept Mr. Stafford from doing anything that would let him break free. After what seemed like minutes, but was probably only a couple of seconds, Mr. Stafford stopped struggling and his eyes glazed over.

Capone broke his bite with an obvious effort of will and tilted his head back. His long fangs glistened from the fresh blood and a bright crimson ring circled his mouth. As I watched, I could see his skin become flush and florid.

Capone turned to look at me. His eyes had a reddish gleam to them and his tongue flicked out between his fangs to lick the blood from his lips. "It's time for you to lose your virginity, Mr. Imbierowicz."

The smell of the fresh blood hit me and overwhelmed my senses. It was like the warehouse from earlier, but even stronger, more powerful. My pulse quickened in anticipation and my fangs grew longer. The sickly-sweet smell of fear that came off of Mr. Stafford awakened a need that I had never felt before. Saliva gushed into my mouth and the scent of the fresh blood was intoxicating. I'd never felt this much excitement when I fed on cow's blood. I wanted to drink deeply from Mr. Stafford, to savor every single drop of his blood. The anticipation of the first taste was even greater than wanting to eat Mom's *rugelach*, my favorite dessert.

Now that Capone had freed himself from Mr. Stafford, the wound on his neck—a raw, circular bite made from all of Capone's teeth—bled freely. There was now a small stream of blood cascading down his neck and I wanted to lick it up.

It'll just go to waste if you don't, Moira's voice purred.

Suddenly, I was standing next to Mr. Stafford, his head pulled back by Capone to neatly expose his neck. I didn't remember moving the few feet toward them; I was just suddenly there. I could hear the slow pulse of Mr. Stafford's blood just under his skin.

I grabbed him by his hair and his arm. As I pulled his neck back further, I could sense Capone backing up a step.

That's it, baby, Moira's voice cooed. *Lick him. Taste him on your tongue. Take a bite of him.*

I leaned forward, my tongue reaching for the sweet blood.

Is my cooking so horrible, scolded Mom, *that you have to resort to this? If you'd rather drink this gentile's blood and disappoint your mother, then go ahead. I won't stop you, but your sister will get all of your Rugelach.*

In that case, drink up, Saul, said Sarah. *More for me.*

Besides, you're really good at disappointing Mom, so go with what you know.

I was less than an inch from lapping up the blood, from sinking my fangs into Mr. Stafford's neck, when I caught the sudden odor of *rugelach*, and a wave of guilt hit me like a ton of bricks. The image of my mother, wearing a blue and white apron and holding a plate of *rugelach,* warm from the oven, filled my head. All my memories of my parents, and how I had failed them, surged through my consciousness.

If there is one force in the universe that a Jewish mother wielded like an avenging angel, it was guilt. I didn't know anybody—from young boys to old men—who wouldn't recoil in fear when faced with a mother's guilt. It was a heavy truncheon that every Jewish mother used to get their children and husbands to behave and to pay attention to them.

Right now, with my mouth poised to bite into Mr. Stafford, and with the smell of his blood stimulating me like a drug, my mother's guilt hit me like a wave of cold water, putting out the fire of excitement and extinguishing the desire of wanting to feed.

I don't want to do this, I told myself. I didn't want to take a life just to satisfy my own hunger. It was wrong, and it would be the final step in making me the monster that Capone wanted me to be.

And that is what he wants, Dad said. *If you feed now, he'll control you. You'll become the monster you've been fighting against all along.*

I was clearly taking too long to feed, and Capone said, impatiently, "Take the bite, Saul. Embrace who you've become. Feel the power that you deserve."

I badly wanted to feed. Mr. Stafford's blood was calling to me.

Sure, listen to your new friend, chided Mom. *What does your poor mother—the woman who raised you from birth—know, after all?*

The guilt was a sharp punch to my gut. I glanced at Mr. Stafford's face. His eyes were still glazed over, but I could see that they were wide with panic and fear. He wasn't struggling, but he was fully aware of what was going on and he knew exactly what was going to happen to him. We both knew that he was going to die. There was nothing that I could do to prevent it, but I wouldn't be the one to take his life from him. That was the one thing that I could control. Ever since the fateful day of the St. Valentine's Day Massacre, I'd felt that my life was no longer mine to control. Whether it had been Bugs Moran, Moira, Agents Truesdale and Wright, Eliot Ness, or Al Capone, somebody else had been controlling my life.

Never again, I told myself.

With every ounce of energy that I could muster, I let go of Mr. Stafford and bolted for the door. I was yelling, "Leave me alone," as I yanked open the door and ran down the hallway. As I ran, all I could hear was the sound of Al Capone, laughing.

Chapter 7

I ran without thought down the stairs and out onto Lake Street, the echoes of Capone's laughter chasing me like the hounds of hell. I ran down the street, under the metal frame of the L, before turning down a side street. My legs felt like rubber and I was exhausted, but I pushed myself to keep running. I had to get away from the monster that I could very easily have become. Suddenly, my feet got tangled up with each other and I collapsed in a heap, tumbling along the hard concrete.

I was drained—both physically and emotionally—and unable to move. The concrete was cold beneath my body and, had I still needed to breathe, I would have been completely out of breath. I just wanted to die. For good this time.

But if you die, then he wins, Dad said.

I pictured Capone laughing as I fled Mr. Stafford's apartment, and I used it to motivate myself to keep going. I dragged my hands along the road, the sting of the fresh scrapes pushing back my exhaustion just a bit. I managed to push myself up into a sitting position. I sat in the middle of the road and looked around. Nobody had followed me out of the building. I was alone, so I figured that Capone hadn't cared enough to chase me. After a minute, I managed to stand up, and though my legs protested at the continued abuse, I started walking down the street.

I came to the corner of LaSalle and Randolph and I was able to get my bearings. My exhaustion was so great now that I was afraid that I'd collapse at any moment. I needed to eat, but I was too scared to return to my apartment. Capone might be waiting for me and, weak as I was, I'd have no chance if I tried stand up to him again.

There was a butcher's shop two blocks to the west. I'd visited it before. It was a small place, run by a Hungarian immigrant and his two sons. Getting blood to feed on was more challenging than you'd think, especially when you were unwilling to take a human life. The stockyards south of town, where Dad worked, were full of vats of the stuff, but I didn't want to go someplace where there was a chance that somebody who knew Dad might see me. *Yeah, that's just what I need, Dad thinking that I'm a ghost and haunting the stockyards.* Instead, I'd made a list of all the butchers who were near my apartment and I went to them.

Not directly, you understand. You can't just go up to a butcher and ask for a bucket of blood. Even with some of the strange foods that the city's immigrants cooked, asking for blood by the gallon would be considered odd.

Each of the butchers collected the blood in buckets before they poured it down the drains. How did I know this? I'd broken into each of them to find out. Well, I really didn't consider it to be breaking in, since it's not like I was stealing anything of real value. They were all just going to throw the stuff out anyway, and I rotated the shops that I visited so that they wouldn't get suspicious.

I'd not been to the Hungarian's place in a couple of weeks, so I knew that it would be safe to stop there. It took me a good thirty minutes to walk the two blocks, as tired as I felt. I went down the alley behind the shops and up to the butcher's door. It was unmarked, as were all the other doors facing the alley, but the odor of blood emanating from behind it was unmistakable.

The door was locked, as expected, but I'd been using a window above the door in order to gain entry. There was a small ledge and the window was usually open to air out the shop. I stood by the door and jumped straight up—and fell about two feet short of the window ledge. I flung my arms out but wasn't able to grab hold of the ledge. I fell with a clatter to the ground, knocking over a trash bin as I landed. The noise was deafening in the alley and I froze, expecting the sound to bring somebody to their window.

I thought I heard a soft chuckle, and Sarah said, *I'm glad to see that your new abilities allowed you to remain as graceful as ever. This reminds me of your* bar mitzvah *during the mother-son dance when you tripped over your own feet and ended up in Rabbi Gershwitz's lap.*

Didn't Mom always say that if you can't say something nice about someone, don't say anything at all? I asked.

Ok, well, that was a really nice loud noise that you made while trying to break into a butcher shop to steal blood. It was so wonderfully loud that it probably woke the whole neighborhood, and now everyone is going to see what an amazing burglar you are!

Oh, give it a rest. I sighed.

Nobody came to investigate, and no lights appeared in any of the windows.

See, nobody noticed, I told Sarah.

Whatever, klutz, came the reply and I could picture Sarah sticking her tongue out at me.

Despite no immediate reaction from the neighborhood I continued to sit there just to make sure. *Did I hear a laugh when I fell, or had that been my sister?* After a few minutes I stood up. I hadn't realized just how drained I was. I concentrated and summoned the last of my strength and jumped again. I still fell short, but I was ready this time and I was able to grab the sill. With a herculean effort, I managed to pull myself up to the ledge. I was panting heavily as I opened the window further and dropped unceremoniously into the shop.

I didn't need to turn on any lights. Even as fatigued as I was, I could still see clearly in the dark shop. Plus, even if I had been blind, I think my nose would have directed me where to go. The smell of blood was strong inside the shop, almost overpowering. I walked over to a corner of the shop where I knew that the butcher kept his blood bucket and picked it up.

Normally I carried a couple of large Thermos bottles to carry away the blood so that I could drink it later. I obviously hadn't brought any of them with me after my flight from Capone, and I was so exhausted and so ravenous that I brought the bucket straight to my mouth and began to drink.

Like a man dying of thirst in the desert I devoured the blood, hungrily, not caring how much I spilled. I felt the cold, slightly congealed blood pour down my throat as I took large gulps of the life-giving liquid. Almost immediately, I felt my exhaustion fall away, like somebody had given me an injection of coffee straight into my veins.

I must have drained half of the bucket before I pulled it from my lips. I felt awake and alive—as alive as a walking dead man could feel—and I let the bucket fall to the floor without thinking. The metal bucket hit the concrete floor with a loud clatter. I could hear the sound of voices coming from upstairs, loud calls being made in a foreign language that I took to be Hungarian. *Sure, you sleep through me knocking over all the trash bins outside, but you wake up at the sound of one little bucket hitting the floor.*

Hey everyone! Come see the best burglar in Chicago! Sarah teased.

A guy can't catch a break.

I had no desire to confront the butcher, so I turned to hurry back to the window above the back door. I had forgotten that I had made a rather large mess while feeding so, naturally, my feet slipped, and I fell with a dull thud into the small pool of blood that had formed on the floor.

Sarah's laughter boomed in my head. *Not one word,* I told her. Amazingly, she kept her trap shut for once. Starting to panic—I didn't want the butcher to see me—I pushed myself up. Trying not to slip and fall again, I moved toward the window.

Just as I reached it and was about to jump, the electric light in the room came on with a sudden, harsh brightness. Somebody—the butcher, I figured—yelled something that I didn't understand, but I heard the unmistakable sound of a shotgun being pumped.

I don't know why, but I turned around. Maybe I was trying to reassure the butcher that I wasn't trying to rob him. As I turned, the butcher gave a cry of pure alarm and terror. I could smell the fear rolling off of him like a cloud of gas. Looking down, I saw that I was covered in blood. In the glare of the light bulb, I could see that my shirt was soaked through with blood, and not just from my fall. I could feel the blood that coated my chin and neck in a sticky mess. Instinctively, I flicked out my tongue to try and remove some of the blood. As I did, my fangs, which had lengthened while I fed, flashed in the light.

There was a clatter and I looked back up to see the shotgun lying on the floor. The butcher was rapidly crossing himself with one hand, while he held the other outstretched toward me and was pushing with it, like he was trying to push me away. He was babbling rapidly, "Vámpír, vámpír," and took several steps backward.

I held up my hands. "I'm not going to hurt you," I said, taking a step forward.

The butcher panicked and yelled as he turned and fled from the room.

You should go tell him you're sorry, Mom said. *And that you'll pay him for the blood. He seemed like such a nice man, and you really don't want to leave him thinking that you're some sort of thief.*

There is no amount of pleading or explaining that I could do to make this better. With a sigh, I turned, jumped to the window, and slipped out into the night. As I ran up the alley, I couldn't help but hear Capone's laughter echoing with Sarah's in my head.

Chapter 8

With reluctance, and quite a lot of trepidation, I returned to my apartment building. I had no other place to go, but I felt much more confident about the thought of facing Capone now that I'd fed. *If he's even still there*, I told myself.

I moved as quietly as I could down the stairs from the roof, and I breathed a sigh of relief as I approached my apartment. I didn't feel the same tingling feeling like I had before, so Capone must have left. I stopped before I reached my door. Mr. Stafford's door was closed. I thought about ignoring it and everything that had happened in there.

You'd let your poor dead neighbor stay hidden in there for who knows how long? Mom chided me. I hung my head. I couldn't ignore it.

Mr. Stafford's door was unlocked, so I opened it and stepped inside. I could smell the lingering odor of cigar smoke that had clung to Capone, as well as the cheap aftershave worn by Nitti. But hanging over it all, like a thick blanket, was the smell of fresh human blood. My fangs jutted out reflexively, even though I'd just fed. I strained to will them back to normal.

Mr. Stafford lay in the middle of his living room. His neck had been torn out and blood coated the walls, ceiling, and floor. Apparently, Capone had just gone ahead and killed my neighbor after I had run out.

Had it been a test? I asked myself. *Was Capone testing me? Was he trying to see just how far I was willing to go?* I looked at the savage hole that he had torn in my neighbor's neck. *Or had this been about something else?*

I shook my head. Whatever the reason, I felt a deep sense of guilt and remorse. My neighbor—a man I'd met only once before—was now dead because of me. Capone may have done the deed, but it was because of me that Capone was here in the first place. *I'd been helpless to resist Capone. I'd been unable to stop him.*

Keep telling yourself that, Sarah said, *It's not like you actually tried. You're really hard on neighbors, aren't you?*

Sarah, leave your brother alone, he feels bad enough without you provoking him, Mom told her. *And don't you use that poor Mrs. Rabinowitz in your insults. She was a wonderful woman who kept an eye on your brother when I couldn't, may she rest in peace.*

Depressed, I walked back out of Mr. Stafford's apartment and over to mine. I unlocked both locks and opened my door, grabbing the small piece of paper as it fell to the floor. That's when I noticed that a calling card had been shoved under my door.

I picked up the card. On the front was written "The Plantation" in a fancy cursive script, with an address down in Hammond, Indiana. Turning it over, I read a short note: "Call on me when you're ready to embrace your true self.—Capone"

I almost crumpled the card to throw it away, but I stopped myself. Instead, I put it in my coat pocket and headed to the phone mounted on the wall in my kitchen. The best thing about my apartment was that I had my own phone—no party line down in the lobby. I picked up the receiver and waited for the operator to come on the line, then gave her the number for Ness.

"Hello," said a very tired—and annoyed—voice when the phone was finally picked up.

"Ness, it's Saul," I said.

"What the hell do you want that couldn't wait until morning?"

"Al Capone just slaughtered my neighbor."

There was a pause, and then a muttered curse came over the line. "What happened?"

I told him about Capone ambushing me outside my apartment, and what had happened with Mr. Stafford. I was really vague about the details of my conversation with Capone, and I completely left out the part about me fleeing and breaking into a butcher's shop. Ness had never asked me where I got my blood from; he only knew that I didn't drink human blood.

It took me about five minutes to explain everything that had happened. Ness was quiet the whole time. When I'd finished, all I heard was a muttered, "Shit" from the other end of the line. Ness was quiet again for about a minute, and then asked, "Did anybody see you go into your neighbor's apartment?"

"Apart from Capone and Nitti, no."

"Good. Call the police and tell them that you heard a commotion that sounded like it was coming from your neighbor's apartment. Have them deal with this."

"Wait, we aren't going to do anything?" I was shocked. "Aren't we supposed to be trying to stop Capone?"

"Yes, we are, which is exactly why we are not going to get ourselves involved in a petty murder investigation. We have more important things to do to get Capone."

"Petty? Tell that to my poor neighbor who is lying dead in his living room with a hole in his neck!"

"Even if the murder charge stuck to Capone, and that would be highly unlikely, who'd believe such a story? Trying to tell a jury what Capone really is would just get you tossed into the loony bin."

I fumed for a bit, but then reluctantly realized that Ness was right. Nobody would believe that Capone was a monster—a real, honest-to-goodness monster. The press and the regular people of Chicago were all willing to accept that Capone was a crime lord—although Capone always denied this—and they would even buy him pulling out a Tommy Gun in order to take care of business, but they'd never believe that he'd rip a man's throat out with his teeth.

"Saul?" Ness asked.

"Yeah?" I replied.

"Call the cops. Let them deal with this. I'll see you at work in the morning."

Ness didn't bother to wait for a reply, and the line went dead. I sighed, feeling even guiltier than I had before about Mr. Stafford's death. Not only was he dead because of me, but his killer would go free because nobody would believe the truth.

Reluctantly, I tapped the plunger on the phone a few times, and then told the operator, "Connect me to the police."

Chapter 9

The police had only asked me a couple of questions when they finally showed up to check on Mr. Stafford. The sergeant who took my statement could tell that I was lying about what I'd heard, but he didn't push the issue. He must have figured that I just didn't want to get involved in what the police were calling "a robbery that had gone horribly wrong". The vast majority of folks in Chicago wouldn't want to be involved in anything like that.

I arrived at work just before 9 o'clock the next morning. Our office was located on the third floor of the federal building downtown, an easy walk from my apartment. It wasn't much to look at, with a large, lackluster main room filled with second-hand chairs and shabby desks that most of the team had to share. Ness had an office to himself at the back of the room behind a glass-paned wall.

I settled into my desk and said good morning to Christian. He mumbled something that I took to be "morning" but he didn't look up from his paperwork. I'd have thought he'd be at least a bit friendlier this morning after I'd saved his life last night, but he seemed determined to keep the status quo. I shrugged and grabbed a pencil and one of the steno pads to begin documenting my own report on the bust at the warehouse. (I'm a horrible typist, so I tried to always write my reports up by hand first before typing them. That saved on forms and carbon paper.)

Ness showed up thirty minutes later, holding a copy of that morning's Tribune. A large headline read: 'Waterfront Still Busted By Police'.

"Good job, men, on the raid last night. It may not have gone according to plan," Friel and Cloonan glared at me from their desks, "but we got the job done."

"But the cops got all the credit," groused Mike King, one of the other members of our team.

"That's fine with me," Ness replied. "I'd like for us to stay out of the papers when we can. We can work better from the background without all the attention from the press." Ness headed toward his office, saying, "Kowalski, I need to see you."

Friel and Cloonan jeered at me, as if I'd been called into the principal's office at school. They were probably hoping that I was going to get reprimanded for screwing up the raid last night. I ignored them since I knew differently, or at least I assumed Ness wanted to know about my encounter with Capone more than he wanted to chew me out for the botched raid.

I followed Ness into his office, shutting the door behind me. He tossed the newspaper onto his desk and took off his suit coat and hat, hanging them both on the only coat rack to be found anywhere within our meager offices. "Tell me about last night," he said, as he sat down.

I remained standing and went over again what had happened when I'd gotten to my apartment. I broke down and told Ness everything about my conversation with Capone this time: all that he had told me about vampires, and his offer to answer my questions about being one. "He said I wouldn't be at my full potential if I didn't feed on human blood."

"And you said that you felt compelled to enter the apartment when Capone ordered you to?"

I nodded, feeling embarrassed about not being able to resist Capone's order. Ness rocked back in his chair, thinking. Finally, he sat upright and looked at me, a quizzical look on his face. "I suppose you won't reconsider feeding on a person."

"No." I didn't hesitate. I had been adamant about this before. Even after Capone's offer to give me the answers I wanted, and the sudden realization that I'd never be as powerful as Capone, or any other vampire for that matter, I still said no. Maybe I'd feel differently if I had wanted to become a vampire in the first place, but I hadn't asked for this to happen to me. I hadn't wanted to become one of the living dead. Refusing to feed on a person was the last hope that I had of holding on to whatever was left of my humanity. Without it, I was nothing more than a monster, just like Capone.

"Not even if they were crooks?" Ness asked. "You know, bad people who probably deserve it?"

I was a bit shocked that Ness was advocating that I commit murder. Even if it made me stronger, and even if it was a crook that maybe deserved it, that didn't change the fact that it was still murder. "No." I said again, stressing the word. I tried to look Ness in the eye, but he was careful to avoid my gaze.

Ness sighed. "Then I guess we'll have to find a way to beat Capone without using a vampire."

"What? Are you firing me?" I bared my teeth, fighting hard to keep my fangs from growing. "Because I have a moral backbone you're going to fire me? I'm still faster and stronger than any of them!" I jabbed my thumb toward the office outside Ness's door. "You wanted me on this team, and now that I won't become your pet monster you're going to kick me out?"

Ness glared at me without meeting my eyes and I stopped talking. "Are you about finished?" I blinked and nodded, feeling both chastised and slightly embarrassed by my outburst.

"You may be all of those things, but if you don't start using that melon between your ears," he pointed at my head, "then I *will* fire your sorry ass. You may be stronger and faster and all that other shit, but if you don't start thinking soon, you're going to get yourself, or one of us, killed." Ness stood up and started pacing behind his desk.

"I respect you for not taking a life so casually. I understand why you didn't do it before, and I think it shows what kind of person you truly are, because you know now that, by refusing to drink human blood, you'll never be as powerful as Capone. It takes a man of strong character to make that kind of decision."

I relaxed a bit and felt my face flush in full embarrassment. I hadn't known just how much Ness really understood about me and my choices.

Ness stopped pacing and placed both hands on the back of his chair. "Sooner or later, you're going to have to decide whether holding onto your humanity is worth the cost. At some point, we all have to make the choice of whether we will kill somebody to save others." He pointed toward the office. "Everybody out there faces those same choices. Maybe they won't become the monster you think you'll become, but they all have to live with the decision to take a life in the service of protecting the lives of others."

Ness sat back down, and I stood there, a bit dumbstruck. "If you aren't going to make the same sacrifices that the rest of the team is willing to make," Ness looked at me with a weary look, "then I don't know what use I have for you. Get back to work and think about that."

I wasn't sure what to think. Ness opened a folder and started to read. I stood there for a moment, then turned to leave, relieved that I hadn't been fired, but concerned about what Ness was asking me to do.

As I turned to the door to make my exit, there was a brief knock, and the door opened. In walked Paul Robsky, the communications guy for our team.

"Hey, boss," Robsky said. "Oh, hi Kowalski," he gave me a quick glance. "Sorry to interrupt, but I just got this, and I figured that you'd want to know about it as soon as possible." Robsky handed a sheet of paper to Ness. I decided not to leave just yet. Robsky was really good at placing wire taps and listening to what people were saying. He's the one who got us most of our intel on what Capone and the other gangs were doing.

"Is this accurate?" Ness asked when he'd finished reading.

Robsky nodded. "Heard it myself. I placed the tap just the other day, so they don't know about it."

Ness nodded and stood up. "Round everybody up. It sounds like we're going to have a busy night."

Chapter 10

"In Our Father's heavenly name, will you please stop that?" Christian said. "You are truly trying my patience."

I stopped drumming my fingers against the edge of the dashboard. I thought about starting back up again, just to spite him, but then thought better of it. Tweaking his nose would just make him even more annoyed at me, and that might lead to us making a mistake. After the problem at the warehouse last night, I was trying hard to be a better agent. It was really hard to do that when we were sitting in a car doing nothing.

Unconsciously, I started to drum my fingers again and Christian glared daggers at me. I stopped again and sat on my hand. "Sorry," I mumbled.

Christian seemed satisfied and turned back to watching the building. It was a three-story brick building located at the edge of Chinatown. The building housed a small factory that made washing machine parts that were used in Chinese laundries across the country, shipping them everywhere by truck. It was the perfect cover for their operation.

Robsky's tap had allowed him to listen in on what the owners were really up to. They smuggled in cases of rice wine, liquor, and beer from China—first through Canada and then across the Great Lakes to Chicago—and distributed it to all the Chinese laundries across the country. It was a slick operation and it might have stayed a secret—all of their communications had been in Chinese, which Robsky didn't understand—but one of the calls had been made to somebody who didn't know a lick of Chinese. They'd had to speak English, and that had been our lucky break.

"Do you remember the plan?" asked Christian for the hundredth time.

I wanted to say something snide—what did he take me for, some kind of *schmendrick*—but then I reminded myself that I was trying to be a better agent. We were only good when we worked together as a team.

"Yes," I nodded, trying to keep the annoyance out of my voice. "When Ness and the others crash the gate,"—Ness had gotten hold of a big snowplow from the city works department—"we'll enter from the back of the building to make sure nobody tries to escape that way."

Christian nodded condescendingly. "It'll be simple," he said, turning to look at me. "Even for you."

"Hey," I said. I wasn't sure if he was joking with me or if he was just being mean. He turned back to stare out the windscreen, so I put my money on the latter. He was becoming more like Agent Truesdale every day. I bit back the retort that I wanted to give him, and instead I asked, "Was it like this for you and Agent Truesdale?" Christian had barely spoken about his former partner after agreeing to work for Ness.

Christian didn't answer my question. "Come on," I prodded him. "I can't picture Truesdale being somebody that would sit around waiting patiently for anything."

"You don't know anything," Christian finally said. "At least he knew when to keep his trap shut."

I ignored the barb. "When Ness convinced you to

work for him, he mentioned that you worked for the Night Watchers."

The statement hung between us, but Christian didn't take the bait and remained silent. "So," I pressed, "what do you guys do?"

"Watch the night, idiot." He continued to stare out of the car's windscreen. I frowned at him.

"Come on, if we're going to take down Capone don't you think I should know more?"

"No."

I blew out a breath and turned to look out the right window. Christian was being purposefully obstinate.

Maybe you should try a different approach? Dad suggested.

Continuing to look out my window, I said, "Did you know that I've never fed on any human blood since I became a vampire?" I turned and saw Christian looking at me.

See, that got his attention.

"It's true," I said, nodding. "I'm afraid of what that would do to me. I figure that if I can avoid drinking human blood that'll mean I'm not fully the monster I've become. That I'm still a bit human."

"So?" Christian returned to looking out the front of the car. "You're still no different than Capone."

"Yes I am. Even according to Capone himself, I'm different."

"What? When did you talk to Capone?"

"Last night. Well, it was probably this morning. He was waiting for me when I returned to my apartment. He told me that the only way I that would become a true vampire would be for me to feed on human blood. As long as I feed on animal blood, I'll never be as strong, or as fast, or as powerful as a true vampire."

"Really?" Christian was looking at me like he'd just learned something new about me, or at least about vampires.

I nodded. "That's what he said, and I have to believe him. He tried to get me to feed. He killed my neighbor right in front of me and offered him to me."

Christian shuddered and I saw him cross himself.

"I was so weak and starving," I said. "I'd not fed since before the raid. The smell, the temptation, it was nearly overpowering."

"What did you do?" Christian asked, actually sounding like he was sincerely interested.

"I ran." I looked down at my hands in my lap, remembering the feeling of terror and powerlessness as I ran. "I ran away as Capone laughed at me."

"But you didn't feed?"

"No." I looked up and looked at Christian, careful to avoid looking into his eyes. "Not on my neighbor. Capone still murdered him, but my conscience is clean."

Christian was silent for a moment. "That must have been hard," he finally said.

"You have no idea," I admitted. "So, maybe you could share some stuff with me since I take it you've learned something new about us vampires."

"I really shouldn't," he started, "as you might use it against us." I started to protest, but he kept talking. "But maybe a little information wouldn't hurt."

I waited, wondering what I'd learn. Everything about being a vampire was new to me, and I wanted to learn everything that I possibly could. Just as Christian was about to talk, we heard the revving of a truck engine followed by two blasts of its horn. Ness's signal. *Damn it.*

Christian leapt out of the car. "Come on, Saul. We've got a job to do." He hurried toward the building, drawing his pistol as he ran.

Maybe next time, I told myself. I opened my door and ran after Christian, passing him to reach the door to the factory first. With a nod from him I pulled on the door, tearing it off its hinges.

Chapter 11

The factory was brightly lit from overhead lights. The bottom floor was a storage and shipping area, with boxes and shipping crates stacked in neat rows. At the far end of the building, we heard a tremendous crash as the snowplow broke through the garage doors.

Panicked cries in both English and Chinese came from the front of the building. A couple of gunshots rang out, which were followed by even more yelling. Christian and I stood our ground, waiting for anybody who was foolish enough to try to make their escape out the back door. Nobody did, so we just stood there waiting, listening to the unseen commotion that was emanating from the front of the factory.

Just as I was beginning to think that this might be an easy bust for us, I heard the sound of running feet coming our way. "Somebody's coming," I warned Christian.

A Chinaman came running down the far aisle. He wore a grey, long-sleeved wool jacket with a straight collar and coiled buttons down the front. Long black hair was braided down his back. I tensed, fully expecting him to turn toward the exit, but he ran on past without a glance at either of us.

Christian pointed in the direction the Chinaman had gone, and said, "Go see what he's doing."

I jogged around a stack of crates to see the Chinaman

kneeling on the ground and bowing, his forehead touching the factory floor. He was babbling rapidly in Chinese. I walked up to him, reaching down with the intent to pull the man to his feet, but I stopped short of touching him as I caught sight of what he was bowing toward.

It was a coffin—an actual coffin—sitting between two long bamboo poles. The coffin was weathered and ancient looking, with many nicks, dents, and scratches along its surface. As I stared, wondering why this Chinaman was talking to a coffin, the lid was lifted from inside by a pale hand. It was quickly followed by a body—a man—who leapt out of the coffin.

I stood there dumbfounded, Capone's words from last night resounding in my head. *Do you sleep in a coffin?*

The man's head was bald along the front, but there was a long, black braid in the back that danced around as he moved. His skin was very pale, and it looked like most of his flesh was scarred or injured, almost like he was in the process of decomposing. He wore a blue, coat-like robe that fell to his knees with long, wide sleeves which hung below his hands. He had loose, tan-colored pants tucked into blue velvet boots. The man noticed me standing there and hurdled over the prostrate Chinaman.

I wasn't sure exactly what this thing was, but it became clear to me that: one, it wasn't a man (at least, not anymore) and two, it wasn't alive. I could even smell the foul odor of decay clinging to it. I prepared to swing at the creature as it landed, but it moved extremely fast—faster than me—and hit me with its left arm.

I was trying to dodge the blow, but it caught me on the side of my head and sent me flying. I landed several feet away and slid into some boxes. My head throbbed from the blow; it was like Rogers Hornsby had hit me out of Wrigley Field on a line drive.

I managed to remain conscious and watched as the creature hopped down the aisle, moving rapidly in five-foot bounds. *Is it hopping? What is this thing, the damned Easter Bunny?*

I got to my feet just as Christian appeared in the intersection. He saw the creature, managed to raise his weapon, and got off a shot. The bullet hit the creature square in the chest, but it seemed to have no effect. There wasn't even any blood coming from the hole that the bullet made.

The creature turned in mid-hop and moved toward Christian. I ran toward them, but the creature was still faster than me. It was a blur of movement even to my enhanced eyes. It got to Christian first, reaching out with a clawed hand. Instead of raking its claws at him, the creature held its hand in front of him and started to speak, whispering words in a language that might have been Chinese, or could have been something else altogether. The effect on Christian was dramatic. He shuddered, as if he'd just been touched by a live electrical wire. His face immediately became ashen and his eyes rolled back up into his head. Despite the severe pain that he was clearly in, I saw him reach for something in his overcoat. *He's probably going for his cross. Does he think that this thing is Catholic?*

I didn't wait to see what would happen. I slammed into the creature, blind-siding it. We fell to the floor and rolled for a few feet before we slammed into a stack of crates. The creature managed to quickly untangle itself from my grasp and stood up, hopping into a smaller space in order to keep itself between me and Christian.

"I don't know whatever the hell it is that you are," I snarled, through my growing fangs, "but nobody hurts my friends."

The creature opened its mouth, revealing cracked and chipped teeth that made it look more like a shark than a person. It let out a slow hiss and a growl and I could smell its rotten, fetid breath. "Feh! Have you ever heard of a breath mint?"

I feinted at the creature with a left-handed jab and then launched a right hook, just like Jack Dempsey. It worked, and my blow smashed into the creature's mouth. Its neck and head twisted briefly with the blow, but then it slowly turned back to glare at me. I sensed a flicker of intelligence, or maybe even some final vestige of humanity, as the creature reassessed my strength.

Still hopping around like some sort of damned pogo stick, the creature lashed out at me with both hands. I managed to block one of them with my left forearm, but the other one twisted and slipped under my other arm to hit me square in the ribs. I staggered under the blow, but I somehow managed to stay on my feet.

We traded a few more blows, but it was faster than me, and apparently more experienced in hand-to-hand fighting. Within a minute, I had a number of bruises and welts all over my head and chest while I'd barely nicked the creature in return. I could hear several cries coming from the front of the building—loud calls coming in Chinese—that seemed to alert my opponent.

As if it had merely been toying with me the whole time, the creature reached out with its hands in a blur of motion that I barely saw and had no chance to stop. Finally pausing from its insane hopping, it grabbed me by my throat and lifted me off the ground. It began to squeeze, the pain unbearable as it began to crush my windpipe. A million hot needles were stabbing at my body—excruciating pain that seemed to envelop me like a wet blanket. My very bones felt like they were on fire. I wanted to scream, but there was no air within me, and the creature's hand on my throat kept any sound from coming out.

At the same time, I noticed that the creature's face seemed to grow new lesions and wounds, and a thick, pus-filled blood oozed out of its eyes and nose. I didn't know what was happening to the creature, but I knew that whatever was happening to it, I was going to die before it finished. My strength was gone, and my vision began to blur. The memory of a similar situation back in February came unbidden to me. I was in the garage where the St. Valentine's Day Massacre had happened. A man in a dark brown suit was holding me off the floor, squeezing the life out of me.

My memory of Mr. Brown—as I had called him back then—must have played tricks on me, or maybe I was losing consciousness, as I swore that I could see Mr. Brown standing directly behind the creature now.

It was no vision. The real Mr. Brown—still wearing the exact same brown suit, slacks, and tie that he'd worn back in February—grabbed the creature and pulled it off of me. He yelled, "Let go of him, you damned Chink!"

I fell to the ground, too weak to stand. I stared in dismay as Mr. Brown grabbed the creature's chin with one hand and the back of its head with the other. With a violent twist, he snapped its head around and tore it completely away from the creature's body. The body fell to the floor in a heap. Mr. Brown casually tossed the head onto the floor after it. Looking at Christian, then back at me, Mr. Brown put a hand up to straighten the brown fedora on his head.

"See ya around, Saul," he said with a smirk. "She'll be happy to know that you're doing well." With that he was gone, running out the back door.

I managed to get to my feet and walk over to Christian, who was leaning heavily against a large crate. "Who in the name of Our Lord and Savior was that?" He pointed after Mr. Brown with his gun.

"I have absolutely no idea," I lied. Mr. Brown's parting words were still ringing in my head. *She'll be happy to know that you're doing well. Who'll be happy?*

Before I could say anything else, I heard the sound of running feet coming toward us. I tensed, trying to summon whatever pitiful reserve of strength I might have left, but then relaxed as Ness and Cloonan came into view. Both looked from us, to the decapitated Chinaman/thing lying dead on the factory floor, and then back to us.

Cloonan let out a low whistle and said, "What in the..." but then trailed off as if words just couldn't describe what he was seeing.

Ness, on the other hand, seemed to take it in stride. "Looks like you two did your job. Good."

Chapter 12

Ness holstered his pistol and turned to Cloonan. "Head up front and make sure that Friel and Gardner have everything under control."

Cloonan continued to glance at the dead body and then to me. I couldn't tell what he was thinking, but I'm sure it was something along the lines of, "How'd a scrawny SOB like Kowalski do *that*?" Ness had to snap his fingers twice in order to get Cloonan's attention.

"Sure," he said, absentmindedly, before he headed back to the front of the factory, shaking his head.

Ness looked at the body, nudging it with the tip of his shoe. "You did this?" he asked.

I considered lying and saying that I had, but I was afraid that my nearly exhausted state might let Ness see right through me. I was also trying to be a part of the team and, besides, my mother had raised me better than that.

"No," I said. Some of my energy was starting to return and I thought that it was possible that I could stand up now without feeling like I was going to collapse. I noticed that some of the color had returned to Christian's face.

Ness looked at me, his eyes a bit wide. He must have thought that I was going to take credit for killing the creature.

"Somebody else killed it," I said. Anticipating Ness's question, I continued. "It was someone that I met in the garage right after the St. Valentine's Day Massacre. I don't know his name, but I call him Mr. Brown. I think he's a vampire, too."

Ness nodded his head, apparently recalling the story that I'd told him in the hospital after Capone had shot me, and unconcerned that there was now yet another vampire to worry about. "Do we know what that thing was?"

I shook my head, but Christian said, "I think it was a *jiangshi*, a Chinese vampire. I've read some stories about them, but I've never encountered one before."

"I'd like to never encounter one again," I added.

Ness finally looked up from the dead creature to look at us. "You look like hell, Wright," he commented.

"Hell is infinitely worse, sir," Christian replied, "but I have definitely been better."

"Do you need some time?" Ness asked.

I started to say yes—I was still woozy after fighting the creature—but Christian said, "Just give us a couple of minutes and we'll be fine."

Ness gave us both a critical look, as if doubting Christian's words, but then nodded his head. "Fine. Take care of this mess before the cops show up. No need to start any rumors." He turned and headed back toward the front of the factory.

We sat in silence for a couple of minutes, my strength slowly returning. I no longer felt dizzy and even managed to walk a few steps without falling over. Christian stood up, finally holstered his pistol, and then said, "Go find a tarp or a box or something to put this *thing* in."

I stopped my pacing and stared at him, heat rising on

my face. "A little gratitude at saving your life—again— would be nice."

"I was dealing with creatures like this long before you came along. I can take care of myself."

"Really?" I could not contain the sarcasm in my voice. "You mean like how you and Truesdale took care of Capone?"

He glared at me. "If you'd just follow orders these things wouldn't happen."

"Oh, so now it's *my* fault that you keep nearly dying?"

"It's *your* fault for not paying attention and acting like a pig-headed imbecile. You aren't thinking like a partner. You just rush around and attack blindly."

"In case you hadn't noticed, my rushing around and attacking blindly just saved your life," I pointed at the body. "Again."

Christian just shook his head; whether it was in disappointment or disgust, I couldn't tell. "You idiot." *Disgust apparently.* He reached inside his coat and pulled out a long piece of paper. It had a bunch of strange writing on it - maybe Chinese. "Had you held onto the creature—pinned its arms—I could have put this on it. It would have immobilized it."

"And just how in the hell was I supposed to know that?" I demanded. "You've not once told me that you had anything like that."

Christian yanked open his overcoat. Inside were several pockets that were sewn into the lining. I could see small bottles, a cross, and what looked like a wooden stake. "Jesus Christ, man," I blurted.

"He is my armor and my shepherd," Christian said with a small grin, "but I also come prepared."

"Have you always carried this arsenal?" I asked.

Christian nodded. I shook my head. "Well, I didn't know that you had anything like this. Maybe if you talked to me I'd actually know about this shit." I waved my hand at the items stuffed into his coat.

Instead of answering me, he just closed his coat. He was too stubborn to admit that I was right. "Let's get this mess cleaned up," he finally said.

I was even more pissed now than I had been before. Not only was he unwilling to admit that I had saved his life—*twice!*—he'd also been keeping what was apparently valuable information from me. He obviously didn't care what happened to me; I was just another monster to him.

"Do it yourself," I said, adjusting my own coat. Without another word, I walked past him and out the door.

Chapter 13

Leaving the factory, I wandered through Chinatown trying to avoid people. I wasn't really thinking about anything, just trying to clear thoughts of Christian out of my head. I couldn't understand where he was coming from, or why he was acting like such an asshole.

He accuses me of not thinking like a partner, I grumbled to myself, *but he's the one who's keeping all the secrets. How am I supposed to know what he has planned? I might be one of the walking dead, but I can't read minds.*

I idly kicked at a tin can, sending it scuttling across an alley. I dug my hands into my coat pockets, turning down the alley. *What's his problem with me anyway?* Ever since Ness and I had met Christian at his apartment, he'd treated me like a *shtik drek. I thought Truesdale was the one who had hated my guts,* I mused, recalling how Truesdale had taken every chance to abuse me. *Christian had always come off as the reasonable guy. Is he mad at me because Truesdale was killed? Does he blame me for his death?*

That didn't make sense. Truesdale had been the one who'd set up the meet with Capone. *I'd been the bait, so how could he blame me?*

I shook my head, crossing some unknown street. I knew the answer, but I didn't want to admit it to myself because it was too close to my own feelings. But that didn't make any sense either. Christian had made it clear enough in the last two months that he considered me to be a monster. That's why he was always acting like a *tuchis* toward me. Maybe some of that was resentment toward me for surviving, while Truesdale had died, but I knew that the real reason was that, to Christian, I was an abomination.

He has to know that I feel the same way, I thought to myself. *He knows that I didn't ask for this. He knows that I also think that I'm a monster. So why can't he just get over himself and at least be polite to me? I'm not asking to be his best friend, just for him to be a normal guy around me.*

I paused at a street corner, finally shaking the thoughts from my head. After a moment of looking around, I realized that I was back in my parents' neighborhood. Mr. Greenbaum's grocery store stood across the street from me, right next to the hairdresser where Mom goes once a month to get her hair done.

I crossed the street and started walking up the block. It was late enough that all the businesses were closed, but as I headed up the road I realized that it wasn't too late. I could hear radios playing and conversations in the warm spring night. I knew that many families would be out on the steps of their tenements, talking about all the mundane things in the world.

I wanted to keep walking up the street. This was my neighborhood; it was where I grew up. I knew everybody on the block, if not by name, at least by sight. I desperately wanted my life to be normal again. Since my death, I had come back home—or as close to it as I could safely get—at least every other week.

With a sigh, I turned down an alley and jumped onto

one of the fire escapes. I climbed up to the roof and jumped across to the next building. Other than some stray cats and birds, I was alone up here. Nobody would see me.

In a few minutes, I stood on the roof of the building across from my parents' apartment. There was a light on in my folks' front room and I knew that Dad was probably reading—maybe finishing the evening paper or a magazine. Mom generally went to bed early, but Dad had always liked to stay up to read.

I wanted so badly to go over there, to open the door and walk in like nothing had happened. "Hey Dad," I'd say. "Whatcha reading?"

"*Oy gevalt*, give your father a heart attack, why don't you? Coming in unannounced like you still live here. Why don't you spend time at your own apartment?"

"Because I want to spend time with you and Mom, that's why."

"Feh!" Dad laid down the copy of *Life* that he'd been reading. "Now you want to spend time with us? Now that your boss has forbidden you to see us, now we are important?" He pointed a finger accusingly at me. "You were determined to get away from us, to make it on your own. Even before you had a job, you spent all of your free time as far away from here as you could get. Then, once you moved out, you never bothered to come home, or even to go to Temple. You chose to stay away except to mooch off of your mother's cooking. Why, we'd never even have known if you were still alive, or anything that you were doing if it wasn't for your nice neighbor, Mrs. Rabinowitz. She knew to keep your mother informed of your goings-on."

"But things are different now," I said, my words

echoing across the empty roof. "I really miss you, and Mom, and even Sarah."

"You didn't miss us before. You had to go and be your own man. See what that got you? A *meshuggeneh* girl-friend who tried to kill you, and the biggest gangster in the country stalking you. Had you missed us enough then, none of this would've happened."

"You don't know that," I argued. I didn't like the point that Dad was making.

"Don't I? Are you saying that your father doesn't know what's going on? I see and hear more than you know. Had you stayed here, like a good son, and respected your mother's and my wishes, do you think you'd have hooked up with that *kurva*?"

"Dad..." Moira hadn't been a whore.

"She was a *kurva*," he cut me off. "I know these things. You'd have been with Edith or Sylvia—they are nice girls—Jewish girls—who your mother and I can approve of. Without that *kurva* you'd not have gotten caught up with Capone or the government. You'd have been here—at home—like a good son."

I turned away from the edge of the roof, shaking my father's words from my head. This same argument always raged in my head whenever I came up here. I really didn't know why I kept coming back. *Am I hoping for something different? Does that make me crazy?*

A raised voice that I recognized cried out, breaking me out of my reverie, "David! Stop it! I don't want to!" It was Sarah! I whirled around in time to see that a Packard sedan had pulled up in front of my parents' building, with her in the passenger seat, and a man, who I assumed was David, in the driver's seat, the engine still running. She must have been on a date. *Good for her! Or, not so good in this case, I guess.* "You just keep your mitts off me, do you hear?"

I bristled, and started to jump down to the street to show this David fellow that he can't mess with my little sister when I heard a sound behind me. It was soft, but it was the unmistakable sound of a foot treading on the tarpaper and gravel roof. On previous occasions, I had thought that I'd heard somebody up here with me, but I had never been able to see anyone. Now it was clear. *Someone is up here on the roof with me.*

I spun back around, straining my ears and scanning the roof. "What the hell do you want?" I demanded. It had to be Capone—or maybe one of his thugs. *Who else could it be?*

From the street, I heard a car door slam, and Sarah yelled "I am *not* that type of girl!" as she stormed off back into the apartment building. David yelled back, "Oh yeah? Well, that's not what I heard, Doll!" before speeding off into the night. I breathed a sigh of relief that she was safe.

There was a familiar-sounding chuckle coming from the far side of the rooftop, followed by more footsteps. A shape finally materialized out of the darkness, some-one my heightened vision hadn't seen.

"Now is that any way to greet an old friend?"

Chapter 14

I stared at the man walking toward me across the roof in disbelief. "Joe?" My co-worker from the Post Office, and my only real friend during my short time working there, stopped a few feet away from me. Joe and I had passed the long hours on the night shift talking about everything from how well the Cubs would do this year, to guessing what was in the letters we sorted. Most of our conversations, though, had centered on our girlfriends. Well, my girlfriend Moira—who had turned out to be a murderous vampire—and Joe's abortive attempts to woo the waitress from the diner, Francine.

I looked around the roof, trying to see if anybody else was here. I expected that Capone was hiding somewhere and was using Joe as bait or something.

"I'm alone," Joe said, pulling out a pack of Morleys. "Nobody else is with me."

"But... what... how?"

Joe chuckled as he plucked a cigarette from the pack. "I see that you're just as articulate as ever." He placed the cigarette between his lips then held the pack toward me. Out of habit, I grabbed one and held it in my hand. Joe opened a book of matches, struck one, and lit his cigarette, the tip glowing red in the darkness. I continued to stare at Joe, taking in his mop of hair and lopsided grin. He held the matchbook toward me and I realized that I had been standing there like a *putz* with my mouth open. I took the matchbook and lit my own cigarette.

"Your folks seem to be doing well," he said, pointing toward their apartment with his cigarette. "Considering all that's happened. And your sister seems to be getting along fine without you around, despite her apparent bad luck with guys."

I was confused. *How did Joe know I was here? Hell, how did he even know I was still alive?* "What are you doing here?" I finally asked.

"What's it look like?" He took a pull from his cigarette, blowing the smoke out like we were on a break at work.

"I mean..." I didn't know what to say, or how to phrase it delicately, so I just blurted. "I'm dead."

Joe looked at me with eyes that I suddenly realized were both very old and very tired. "I know. I saw the short piece in the paper. I've been dead before, too."

Wait? What? I was silent, but the sly grin that Joe gave me made it clear that my mouth had fallen open again.

"I'm a vampire," he said, matter-of-factly.

Wait? Joe is a vampire? But... My mind wasn't keeping up with the conversation. "A vampire? Have you always been a vampire?"

Joe gave a short laugh, "Of course not, you idiot. I started out life as a man, just like you."

"No, damn it," I cursed, my anger burning through my confusion. "At the Post Office. Were you always a vampire when we worked there?"

"When *you* worked there," Joe countered in the argumentative tone he used whenever we talked about sports, or dames, or anything, really. "I still do. You should see the *schmo* that Mr. Dickenson hired to replace you. He doesn't like baseball—can you believe that?—or any sports. And he's married and doesn't care about talking about dames or anything. Getting through a shift with him is complete hell."

"What?"

"You know, Francine misses you. After you died she finally agreed to go out with me. I think it was out of sympathy at first, but we hit it off. We've been dating—"

"Damn it," I interrupted him. "How long have you been a vampire?"

Joe sighed, taking another drag on his cigarette, stalling for time. He stared over the edge of the roof, not really looking at anything. I was getting impatient, but before I said anything else, he finally spoke. "I don't like to talk about it." He turned to look at me, though I could tell that he was being careful to avoid looking direct-ly into my eyes. "I've done a lot of unspeakable things. Things that, if I ever do die, will surely earn me an eter-nity in hell."

He finished his cigarette, flicking the butt to the roof and stepping on it. "I was born in 1730, and I died twen-ty-two years later. I've been a vampire ever since."

"Nearly two hundred years," I said quietly, a bit in shock. Joe nodded.

"But this is great," I said. Joe gave me a quizzical look. "Don't you see? I have so many questions and now you can answer them. Capone has offered to teach me, but I'm not willing to pay his price of admission. But you, you can tell me everything."

"You don't want to learn anything from me," he said. "And you're smart to stay away from Capone. He's dangerous."

"That's why I need your help. I need to know how I can stop Capone. How to take him down."

Joe shook his head wearily. "If you were smart, you'd get out of town. That's why I finally showed myself to you tonight."

"Get out of town? Why?"

"There's a war coming," Joe sighed, turning to put his foot on the edge of the roof, staring down into the street.

"Damn it, Joe. What in the hell are you talking about? I don't care about any stupid war. Why won't you help me?"

"That's what I'm trying to do, you dolt. I'm not talking about another war like the one that was fought over in Europe. No, this is a vampire war. And if you're smart, you'll get out of town. Like I am."

"You're leaving? I just found you, you can't leave."

"Like hell I can't. You want to know why I've lived to be almost two hundred years old?" I nodded my head dumbly. "It's because I don't stick my neck out for anybody. When things get too hot, whether it's from harassment from vampire hunters or from the arrival of more powerful vampires, I bug out. I don't stick around. Which really sucks, 'cuz I think the Cubs might have a chance to take the pennant this year."

I stared at Joe, wondering what to say. I just found out that my best—my only—friend is a vampire, and I learn that he is running away. It wasn't fair, and I was starting to get mad at everybody and everything. My supposed partner hates my guts, my family thinks that I'm dead, and my best friend is abandoning me.

"Fine," I blurted. "Run away, you *shvuntz*."

Joe shook his head. "Come with me," he said. "It won't be safe here when the war starts, especially for a *vegan* like you."

"A what?"

"A vampire who hasn't reached his full potential—a vampire who hasn't fed on human blood."

"See?" I pleaded, extending my arms to Joe. "That's why I need you to stay. To tell me things like that."

Joe shook his head. "I'm planning to be on a train to Kansas City before dawn. Why don't you come with me?"

"I can't leave."

"Why not?"

"I've got a job, and I won't leave my family behind."

"You can get another job," Joe countered. "And your family thinks that you're dead. You've already left them behind."

His remark stung, because it was true. I was dead to them, and I'd never risk hurting them again by showing up not dead on their doorstep.

"Look," Joe said, "if you come with me, I can answer all of your questions. You won't have to be in the dark anymore about who, and what, you are."

I looked across the road. The light in the front room was out now. Dad had gone to bed while Joe and I had been talking. *What do I have here that's worth staying for?* To my parents, I was dead and buried. I didn't have a girlfriend, or any friends, for that matter. There was my job with Ness, but would he really miss me? I knew that none of the others on the squad would miss me. Christian would probably rejoice and praise the Lord with me gone. There really was nothing left for me in Chicago.

Chapter 15

I turned to look at Joe. "You said a vampire war was coming?"

Joe nodded. "Somebody is getting ready to challenge Capone's hold on the city. I don't know who they are, but I know they're trying to make new vampires to fight for them, and they are recruiting any vampire to join them. They're even bringing in vampires from as far as China."

"Well, they may be disappointed about that. I ran into a Chinese vampire tonight, but he ended up dead."

Joe's eyes widened at that news. "How did—"

I cut him off. "I didn't kill it. There was another vampire there, somebody I call Mr. Brown, who killed it. He saved my life."

"Are you working for him?"

I shook my head. "Uh-uh. The first time I met him, he tried to kill me. I've not seen him again until tonight." Thinking back to the fight with the *jiangshi* I started to wonder why Mr. Brown had bothered to save me at all.

"Well, if Mr. Brown isn't working for Capone..." Joe began, and I again shook my head in response. He continued, "Then his master is probably the one who's preparing to take on Capone. If they go to war, it won't be safe for anybody, no matter if they're supernatural or normal. That's why I'm leaving while I can, before everything gets too dangerous."

"You said they were making new vampires as well as trying to recruit them?" An idea was starting to form in my head.

"Yes. Whoever is doing this knows that they'll need foot soldiers to take on Capone, and not your run-of-the-mill Italian or Irish immigrants looking to get in with the gangs. They want vampires."

"But doesn't Capone have his own vampires?"

Joe nodded. "Sure, but he's always kept the number of them that are close to him small. He doesn't trust too many people, and those that he does, he likes to keep control of them. It's hard to control a vampire, even one that you've created."

I thought back to how Moira had betrayed Capone, trying to create vampires for Bugs Moran so that she could get out from under Capone's grip. It made sense that Capone would want to keep control of everything himself. A new thought occurred to me.

"So, if Capone doesn't have many vampires working for him, and he knows that a war is coming, he might try to recruit his own vampires?"

Joe nodded hesitantly. "I suppose that makes sense."

"Of course it does," I said. "That's why he tried to recruit me."

"What do you mean?"

"The other night Capone came to my apartment. He killed my neighbor, Mr. Stafford, and he wanted me to feed on him. Capone said that he'd answer all of my questions and help me learn how to be a real vampire."

"You don't want to learn anything from Capone. I said it before, you're smart to stay away from him."

"I want to take Capone down for what he's done to

me. If he's recruiting me to help fight for him, that could be a way for me to get close enough to Capone so that I can take him down."

Joe was shaking his head. "That's crazy. He won't be doing anything to help you."

I ignored Joe, my mind already racing ahead with the idea. I'd let Capone recruit me, and I'd finally get my chance to kill the bastard.

"Saul!" Joe yelled at me. "Whatever you're thinking, it won't work. You're a *vegan*, so even if Capone does let you get close to him, you don't have the strength to kill any full vampire, let alone Capone. And if you feed on a human that Capone has just fed on, then he'll be your master and have power over you. You'd be a full vampire, but you'd still be unable to do anything to him."

"How would he be my master if he didn't create me?"

"A vampire's master isn't just dependent on who made them. The bond is created when the new vampire feeds for the first time, by sharing the meal with the master."

"I've fed before."

Joe shook his head impatiently again, sighing, and looking at me like I was a child. "Not on a person."

"Why does everybody keep trying to get me to eat people?"

"The only way you could have enough power to defeat Capone is if you feed on a person by yourself, without Capone or anybody else feeding before you. You'd be your own master and unable to be controlled."

"Like you?" I asked.

"No," Joe said quickly, looking both angry and sad at the same time. "I had a master, but he's been dead for a long time." He looked back at me. "If you're unwilling to feed on a person, then you'll never have the power to defeat Capone."

"So, I have to become a monster in order to defeat one." I sighed. "I'm not willing to commit murder to stop a murderer."

"Haven't you heard anything I've been saying? You don't have to kill them," Joe said, the exasperation clear in his voice. "You just have to feed on them. But you have to be careful. Human blood is potent. It's like a drug—once you have it, you want more. Once you start feeding, you won't want to stop and, if you can't resist, before you know it, the person has died."

I turned away from the edge of the roof, wondering how else I could get Capone. I looked back at Joe, a new idea forming in my head. "You could do it."

Joe's eyes widened as he understood what I was talking about. "Uh-uh." He held up his hands and waved them dismissively. "I told you that I'm leaving. I'm not going to get involved."

"But you *could* do it," I persisted. "You said your master is dead, so Capone couldn't control you, and you're a full vampire, so you'd have the strength to do it." I was really starting to like this idea.

"No, Saul. I won't do it."

"But why?" I protested. "Why won't you help me? Are you afraid? A *shvuntz*?"

"No!" Joe yelled and, for a second, I was afraid. I could feel the force of the word hit me and I saw the real Joe, something that was not my friend. Long, sharp fangs jutted from his mouth and his face took on a gnarled, demonic look. His eyes blazed with a feral, red glow.

"You know nothing about me." He spit the words at me. "I won't be used by anyone ever again." He pointed in the general direction of downtown. "I plan on being on a train in a couple of hours and leaving all of this behind." Joe's voice softened at the end and his features returned to normal. I wondered what Joe was, because he was different than what Capone, Mr. Brown, and Moira had looked like as vampires. Joe was wilder, more monstrous, like a creature straight out of a nightmare.

Joe turned and gripped the edge of the roof. "Please, don't ask me again. I have my reasons for not helping you." He turned back to look at me, very much the old Joe that I had known. "I gotta go, Saul. If you want to come with me, meet me at Union Station at five. If not, then I wish you the best of luck. You'll need it."

Before I could say anything else, he leaped over the edge of the roof. I ran forward and saw him float almost effortlessly down to the ground. He landed softly and looked back up toward me. He gave me a small salute and then was gone, disappearing into the shadows so fast that I couldn't even see him.

Chapter 16

I paused in front of the door, my hand raised to deliver a knock, but I hesitated. I hadn't been here since early March when Ness had brought me along to recruit Christian. Christian had agreed to work for Ness, as long as he only had to deal with me at work. He didn't want to have anything to do with me outside of work, and he had made it abundantly clear that he didn't consider me a friend. I had kept away, hoping that would help our working relationship. It hadn't, but I had respected Christian's wishes. *Not that he appreciated it.*

Now I was about to knock on his door to ask him for his help, and I was afraid that my being here without his permission would set him off. If he got mad and refused to help me, then I couldn't pull off what I was planning.

I swallowed and tried to make myself stand in a non-threatening manner. I smiled and, with my heart in my throat, I knocked on the door. I could hear a chair being slid back and the pad of feet coming toward the door.

Christian opened the door partway, standing so as to block anybody from entering his apartment. He wore slacks, a white shirt, and brown suspenders. He'd not yet put on his tie. I caught the smell of freshly cooked eggs, toast and butter, and coffee coming from his kitchen. He'd looked bored, and a little bit annoyed, when he'd opened the door, but when he saw who had interrupted his breakfast, his expression changed to anger and hatred.

"What on earth are you doing here?" he spat. "I told you to never come here again!"

"I need your help," I said, trying to sound apologetic.

"Well, you won't get any help from me. Get out of my building." He stepped back and started to slam the door shut.

I moved quickly, shoving my foot over the threshold. Despite Christian's desire to keep me out, his original invitation meant that I could still enter his home. I guess once you give someone an invitation, it can't be rescinded. That worked in my favor and my foot kept the door from being closed. There was a dull throb in my foot as the heavy door bounced off of it. Christian grabbed the door and tried to force it closed.

"I said get out, you monster," he grunted with effort.

I had stopped by my apartment after my encounter with Joe and had fed before coming here. I wasn't feeling any of the effects from the *jiangshi*, so it took no effort for me to push the door open all the way. Christian stumbled backwards under my push and I stepped into the apartment, closing the door behind me.

"Look, Christian," I said. "I really need some help and—" I couldn't finish the sentence. Sharp, burning pain flared on my face and neck and I gasped, instinctively holding up my arms to shield me. Christian stood in the little hallway, his arm moving to fling more liquid at me from a small vial. He held a large wooden cross in his left hand, brandishing it at me. "In Jesus' name, I command you to leave this place." He flung even more liquid at me, several drops burning into my hand and cheek where they struck me.

"That hurts," I said. "Are you throwing holy water at me?" I stepped forward and grabbed for the vial, but Christian was surprisingly quick and jumped back, thrusting the cross in my face.

"Stop that!" I grabbed for the cross, but he pulled it away from my grasp. "I keep telling you that crosses don't work on me. And how does your holy water work when your cross doesn't?"

"The water's been blessed by a Rabbi, idiot. Be gone, spawn of Satan!" He flung the last of the holy water at me, which burned and stung where it hit me, but I didn't budge.

"Since the cross doesn't work, maybe this will." Christian reached into the pocket of his trousers and pulled out a silver object that glinted in the light of the hallway. He thrust it at me, and I saw a silver disc with the six-pointed Star of David etched upon it, painted in a brilliant blue. "The power of God commands you to leave," he said, in passable Hebrew.

I instinctively flinched a little at the sight of the holy symbol, but I was surprised to find that I felt nothing. No pain, no desire to leave, just a building annoyance. I placed my hands on my hips and glared at Christian. "Are you done playing games? Can we talk now?"

Christian looked at the Star of David in his hand and thrust it at me again, then a third time. When I still didn't budge, he finally said, "Why isn't this working?"

"I don't know," I admitted. "Maybe it's because you aren't Jewish. Or maybe it's because I'm a *vegan*."

"A what?" Christian stared at me.

"It's what somebody who's not a full vampire is called."

"Where did you learn that from? Have you been consorting with more monsters like you?"

"I haven't been consorting with anybody," I said, sounding haughty. I really wasn't sure as I didn't know what consorting meant. "A friend told me."

"Another monster."

"Hey, Joe's not a monster," I said, quickly defending him, though the image of his face as it twisted into the cruel form with fangs jutting out flashed in my mind and gave me pause. *Is he?* I ignored the thought. "He's a friend, and he's no longer in town. He got on a train this morning and left Chicago."

"What kind of friend is he if he left you?"

I paused, as I'd been wondering the same thing, but I didn't want Christian to know that I was thinking the same thing that he was. "Joe is my best friend. Hell, he's my only friend. He left because he said there's a war coming. A vampire war between Capone and some other vampire that wants to take Capone down."

This seemed to peak Christian's curiosity as he lowered the Star of David.

"That's right. Somebody is muscling in on Capone's turf and is trying to take him down."

"Good. They'll do our job for us, then."

"No." I was shocked that Christian didn't seem to understand. "A war between vampires will get out of hand. All sorts of innocent people will get killed. And if this other vampire is strong enough to take down Capone, do we really want somebody like that to be in power?"

Christian lowered his head in thought, and then shook it. He turned and walked into the living room and plopped down in his armchair. I followed him and sat down in the other chair.

"Look," I said, "we know what a war between normal gangs can be like. Remember what happened in '26 when Hymie Weiss shot up Capone's hotel over in Cicero? I don't want to know how much bloodier a war between vampires would be."

"They're really bad," Christian allowed. "Have you ever heard of the Boma Epidemic?" I shook my head. "Boma was the administrative capital of the Belgian Congo until a few years ago. During the Great War, two vampire factions from Europe tried to take control of the Congo in order to profit from the war. It was a bloody event that lasted for months. The Belgians were not in a state to do anything about it, other than trying to keep the news of the killings from getting into the press. They said it was an outbreak by an unknown disease to explain all the deaths, and the normal press didn't look twice. But the Night Watchers knew what really happened. That's part of the reason that Truesdale and I were in Chicago looking for leads on vampires. We couldn't let a similar thing happen here."

"So you know why it's important to keep a vampire war from starting."

Christian nodded. "Letting two vampire gangs fight for control of Chicago would be a disaster. But what can we do about it? We aren't able to keep them from fighting if they really want to. We don't have the men or the resources to do that."

"We have one resource you Night Watchers never had." Christian looked at me quizzically. "Me," I said, jabbing my thumb at my chest.

"You're not a resource, you're just another monster."

I ignored the comment. "Remember how I said that Capone had tried to get me to feed on my neighbor the other night?" Christian nodded. "I don't think he was just trying to get me to feed. I think he was trying to recruit me. He wants me to help him prepare for the coming war. I also think that's what Mr. Brown was doing last night; he was trying to get the Chinese vampire to side with his master."

"Then why did he kill it?"

I shrugged. I didn't know and it seemed irrelevant to me. "What matters is that both sides are recruiting foot soldiers."

"And how can you help to stop this?"

"By joining Capone."

Chapter 17

Christian laughed. Not a short chuckle, but a deep belly laugh that seemed to consume his entire body. He kept laughing, tears forming in his eyes. I did my best to glare at him to get him to stop. I mean, I was serious and I didn't think that this was at all funny.

After a couple of minutes, Christian finally calmed down, wiping the tears from his eyes. "You can't be serious," he finally said.

"Of course I'm serious," I retorted.

"How does you joining with Capone stop a vampire war?"

"It doesn't," I admitted, but quickly added, "but it gets me close enough to Capone so that I can stop him."

"If you can."

"I can take Capone down," I said with more conviction than I felt. Joe's words echoed in the back of my mind, *if you're unwilling to feed on a person, then you'll never have the power to defeat Capone.* I wasn't about to tell any of this to Christian, though. If he suspected that I couldn't do what I said that I could, he would never support my plan. I still wasn't willing to kill anyone in order to become a full vampire, but I'd been able to kill Moira, and I wasn't even a vampire then. If I got close to Capone, I was sure that I could kill him, too.

Christian must have believed me because he didn't

question my statement. He sat in his chair, rubbing his chin for a moment. Finally, he said, "So you'd be able to get close to Capone, and you'd then be able to kill him."

I nodded, excitement spreading up from my stomach.

"Are you a complete idiot?" And my feeling came crashing down, replaced by a growing anger. "You'd replace a monster we know about, and can contain," Christian accused, "with a monster we know nothing about. How is that an improvement?"

I relaxed a little, as I had given this some thought. Now I would show Christian that I wasn't the idiot that he thought I was.

"Capone is bound to know who is trying to take him out. By getting on the inside, I can learn who that is. Then, taking down Capone removes him from the picture *and* removes the threat of the vampire war. Without Capone around, this other vampire won't have any reason to go to war. That means that we can then focus our attention on this other vampire and take him down as well, without all the violence that an all-out vampire war would bring."

Christian gave this some thought, and I knew that he was going to try to pick it apart. Before he could say anything, I added, "It may not be perfect, but it's better than using a civilian as bait to lure Capone into the open to try to shoot him." Christian flinched at that, as I had intended. Truesdale's plan to try to kill Capone by using me had been both risky and foolish. I hoped that by reminding Christian of that, it would get him to see that my plan would work. *Now to seal the deal.*

"This is why I need your help. You have the experience to make sure that the plan works. Without you, this won't work, and a lot of innocent people will die."

Christian sighed and fingered the little silver cross that he wore around his neck. "It's far from perfect, and there's a good chance this will blow up in our faces."

I could feel the excitement and hope building in me again. I leaned forward in the armchair.

"But I will help you, on one condition," he held up a finger.

"Yes?"

"This doesn't change anything between us. I'm still not your friend… but I can be your partner. Sometimes it takes a monster to stop a monster."

I gasped, ignoring the subtle slur. I hadn't expected him to actually agree with my plan.

"So what's the next step?" Christian asked.

"First, we can't let Ness know. If he finds out, he'll put a stop to it in a heartbeat."

Chapter 18

It was late afternoon when I walked into the lobby of the Lexington Hotel. Christian and I hadn't gone into the office today, spending the morning working out our plan. That had prompted a call from Ness wondering where Christian was. He'd lied to Ness that the attack by the *jiangshi* was still bothering him, and that he'd need a couple of days to recover. Ness hadn't asked about me, which was no surprise; he knew how Christian felt about me. Ness would probably be as amazed as I was that we were actually working together.

I walked across the hotel's lobby and took a seat in an oversized leather armchair near the front desk. A group of men were playing a game of billiards golf on the hotel's rectangular green. By the way they were acting, I figured that the iced teas and lemonades they were drinking were probably spiked with something stronger. I lit a cigarette and opened the copy of the Tribune that I'd brought with me.

Christian had insisted on keeping our plan simple. I think it was because he didn't trust me to handle anything really complex, but that was fine by me. I'd meet with Capone and convince him that I wanted to work with him. I didn't think that would be too hard to do, since he'd already tried to recruit me. Then, I just needed to find out who was trying to muscle in on Capone's turf. That might be a bit harder to do, but I figured if I could get Capone talking, the name would come out.

I was starting on my third cigarette and still pretending to read the paper when I finally saw the man I had been waiting for. It wasn't Capone—I hadn't expected to see him coming or going through the main lobby of the Lex—but it was the next best thing.

Frank Nitti had just entered the lobby from the main entrance. He wore a slick suit of a light cream color and a pale blue shirt underneath. He walked over to the group that was playing billiards golf, chatting with them and trading a few jokes. Nitti left them to their game and headed toward the elevator. I got up to follow him.

If I had hoped to surprise him—which I hadn't—it wouldn't have worked. As I got closer, the two men standing by the elevator flinched, their hands moving toward the weapons they had hidden inside their jackets. Nitti saw the move and turned around to see who was trying to sneak up on him. He gave me an appraising look at first, probably deciding if I was really a threat or not. After a moment, he gave a slight nod of recognition, and a thin sneer of a smile crossed his face. He held up a hand, signaling the goons behind him, who pulled their hands away from their jackets. Nitti stepped toward me, and I could smell the pomade that he used to keep his hair neatly parted down the middle of his head.

"Mr. Imbierowicz, isn't it?" He spoke with confidence, and only the slightest hint of an Italian accent.

The last time I'd seen Nitti, he'd been offering my neighbor to Capone for him to feed, and to try to entice me. The time before that, he'd shot at me. Looking at me now with cold, grey eyes, I wasn't sure if he wanted to shoot at me again.

"I want to see your boss."

"And what makes you think he wants to see you?"

I was taken aback by this. I had expected that Capone would want to see me. My surprise must have shown, because Nitti gave a soft laugh, like I'd been the butt of some joke.

"He wanted to see me before," I finally said, though it sounded lame even to me. Maybe if I hadn't already fallen on my face, so to speak, it would have sounded better.

Nitti didn't say anything, just turned and continued toward the elevator. I hesitated for a moment, which I'm sure was the point; just one more way to take a jab at me. I quickly followed him, though, and the two goons guarding the elevator didn't move.

We rode the elevator up to the fifth floor in silence, Nitti staring at me like I was some animal in the zoo. I tried to stare back, but he didn't seem to care. When the doors slid open, Nitti walked out and down the hall with me following him—without any hesitation this time. He opened a door off the wide hallway and we entered what looked like a sitting room. Nitti finally broke his silence, saying, "Wait here," before opening another door.

There were a few chairs along one wall, but I didn't feel like sitting. I expected Nitti to be back soon. I wasn't disappointed. He was only gone for maybe a minute when the door opened again and he came out and walked past me. From the doorway, Al Capone said, "Won't you please come in, Mr. Imbierowicz?"

Chapter 19

I walked into Capone's office as he returned to sit behind his large desk. I could hear the traffic down on Michigan Avenue as I walked across the plush carpeting. A cigar sat smoking in a cheap glass ashtray on Capone's desk. The room was large, but not as nicely furnished as the office at his home.

Capone was wearing a pale green silk shirt with a green and white-striped tie. He picked up the cigar and pointed at a chair in front of the desk. "Have a seat, Saul."

I moved to sit down, hoping that it would hide my nervousness. Capone had always referred to me as "Mr. Imbierowicz" before, and the only other time that he'd used my first name, was when he killed my neighbor and tried to get me to feed upon him. Taking my seat, I looked at Capone, careful to not stare directly into his eyes. I wouldn't be fooled into doing that again.

"You came here without that fool, Ness, so this isn't an official visit." Capone leaned back in his chair and took a drag on the cigar. He let out a cloud of bluish smoke. "Are you here to take me up on my offer, or is there another reason?"

"The other night you said you could provide me with answers."

"I still can."

"Even if I'm a *vegan*?" I had been watching Capone

closely, hoping for a reaction to showing him that I'd learned something, but his face was as still as a death mask.

"You try to impress me with some tidbit you've picked up from somewhere. Maybe from a cockroach who's scurried to hide when the light has come on."

I tried to keep my own face just as impassive. I wasn't sure how Capone had known about Joe, or if he hadn't and he was just toying with me. By the way that he smiled, I had apparently failed to keep my own emotions in check.

"It's obvious that whoever told you this isn't around anymore, otherwise you wouldn't be coming to me now."

"My boss and the guys I work with don't understand. Hell, most of them don't even know who I really am. They can't help me learn about what I have become. The only person who could've—besides you—left town this morning." I figured it was good to let Capone know that Joe had left town. Hopefully that would keep Capone from looking for him.

"I seem to recall that the other night you didn't want my help. You ran away, like a scared child into the night." He gave me a malicious grin. "You know the price if you want to get any answers from me."

"I'm not going to kill anybody."

Capone sneered at me. "Stupid *vegan*. You think that you can keep your morals even after you've died? If your friends knew the truth, do you think they'd embrace you?"

"I don't know," I admitted. "But I won't take anybody's life."

"Then I have no use for you. Slink back to your idiot

boss." Capone flicked his hand in a dismissive gesture, ash falling from the end of the cigar.

Christian had expected that Capone might react this way, so I was prepared for the rejection. "I know there's a war coming."

"Who are you, James Good? I thought you worked for the Treasury Department, not the War Department."

"A vampire war," I stressed.

"I don't know what you're talking about," Capone said, deadpan.

I blinked a couple of times, not sure how to respond.

"Whoever told you that sold you a bill of goods. Certainly, there's nothing going on in *my* town that's a threat to *me*." Capone gave me a hard look, and I was sure that he was including Ness in that statement. Christian and I hadn't covered this possibility, figuring that Capone would accept me joining him solely because of his earlier interest. I was starting to panic, wondering what I could say to convince Capone that I should be here.

"Then you were aware that a *jiangshi* was brought into town yesterday." Capone actually raised one eyebrow slightly, which gave me all the encouragement that I needed. "Somebody was there to meet it, and it wasn't one of your men. I took it out, though."

"You?" It was clear by his tone that he didn't believe me. I just nodded, not trusting myself to speak and reveal the lie.

"If you insist on remaining a *vegan* I have no use for you," Capone repeated.

"I'm willing to tell you what Ness has on you," I blurted. I was getting desperate.

Capone laughed. "Your boss doesn't scare me. I'm a

respected businessman in this city, and Ness can't prove anything to the contrary. Good day, Mr. Imbierowicz." Capone pressed a button on his desk and I heard the door open behind me. I got up, reluctantly, and headed toward the door where one of Capone's flunkies was waiting.

"Come back when you decide to grow a pair and actually want to learn what I can teach you," Capone said in parting.

The flunky walked me out of the sitting room and into the hotel corridor. As we walked toward the elevator, we passed an open door. Frank Nitti was inside; I could smell his pomade from the hallway. We passed the doorway quickly, but I could make out a bit of the conversation.

"...and make sure the guys get to the plantation early tomorrow. The boss wants to make sure everything goes smoothly for the party."

"And the guests of honor?" asked another voice.

"Make sure we have a car ready, and a reliable driver. They won't be in any shape to do anything ever again."

The rattle of the elevator doors opening drowned out the rest of the conversation. The flunky gestured for me to enter, and I had no chance to hear any more. When we reached the ground floor, the flunky stayed in the elevator but motioned for me to leave. Outside, the two goons watching the lobby eyed me until I left and started walking toward the door.

I had failed to learn anything. Unless I was willing to kill somebody for Capone, I had just blown our only chance to find out anything useful.

Chapter 20

"My Lord and Savior!" exclaimed Christian. We were sitting in a booth at a nondescript diner a few blocks from the Lexington. "Can't you even do a simple task? The man clearly wanted you, and you can't convince him to bring you into the fold?"

"Geez, calm down," I said. "I tried everything, okay. I even mentioned the stuff from yesterday, but he wouldn't bite."

"Because you won't bite," he said sourly. The waitress came over to refill our coffee.

"You two lookin' to order anything?"

"No, thank you, ma'am," Christian smiled politely. "Just the coffee for now."

She gave us a sideways look, but refilled our cups and returned to the counter.

"Yes," I said, answering Christian's reproach. "I won't stoop to his level just to get on the inside. We'll think of another way."

Christian grunted as he poured sugar into his coffee. I sighed and reached into my coat pocket to pull out my lighter. As I did so, my hand flicked over the edges of a card. I pulled it out and saw it was the card that Capone had left under my door. I had put it into my coat that morning after cleaning myself up and dealing with the cops. I read his note and gave a silent laugh, tossing the card onto the table. It landed note side down.

I picked up my cigarettes and pulled one out, lighting it with my Ronson. I blew out a stream of smoke toward the ceiling. Christian was still absently stirring his coffee.

"We'll think of something," I said.

"Right."

"Come on, man. This is just a setback. Are you telling me that you and Truesdale never had any setbacks?"

"You mean before we met you?"

I winced at the jab and picked up my own coffee. I idly wondered about the coffee and the cigarette. I was the living dead. I didn't need to eat or drink anything except for blood, yet I had been craving the cigarette and the coffee had the taste that I wanted. *How was that possible? Why did it happen? How can I still taste things, or crave things, when I'm dead?*

Are you willing to kill some schmo *just so you can learn the answers?* Dad asked.

You know the answer to that, I responded, but I was getting tired of not knowing all of these things.

"We need to go to the office tomorrow," Christian said absently. "Ness won't buy that the *jiangshi's* attack is still bothering me after two days."

"What for?" I asked in irritation. "All we do is nip at the edges of Capone's organization. We've never done anything that hurts him. Hell, he told me today that he doesn't see Ness as a threat. So why are we even bothering?" I picked up the card and started to nervously turn it between my fingers.

"You know why," Christian said with an exasperated sigh. "Ness and the others have explained it to you enough."

"They're just afraid that Capone will beat any charges that they manage to bring against him." I paused, looking at the front of the calling card.

"Do you blame them? We need an airtight case against Capone and, even then, we have to make sure that the prosecutor, judge, and jury aren't bought off."

"What if we have a witness?" I was looking at the name on the card. *The Plantation.*

"A witness to what?"

"Murder."

"What are you talking about?" Christian asked in annoyance. "Whose murder?"

"I don't know," I admitted. "Something I overheard when I was leaving the Lexington. Frank Nitti was telling some of Capone's men to be at the plantation early tomorrow."

"The plantation?"

"Yes." I held up the card. "*The Plantation.* It's down in Hammond, Indiana. From what Nitti was saying, Capone is throwing a party there tomorrow night."

"So?"

"So, the guests of honor are going to be killed there," I said in an excited whisper.

"Nitti said that?" The doubt was clear in his voice.

"Well, not in so many words," I admitted. "But he said that they wouldn't be in any shape to do anything… ever again."

"That's kind of thin."

"Bullshit. It's no thinner than what you and Truesdale had when I led him onto the bridge for you."

"I told him that we were moving too quickly," Christian said under his breath, though it was clear to me.

"Look, I know it won't be easy –"

"Nothing ever is with you."

I ignored the comment. "But if I can get into the dinner, or at least into the building, and I can see what happens, then I can be a witness. I'm a government agent, so I'd be a credible witness."

"Won't Capone know you're there? Both he and Nitti know what you look like, and don't you monsters feel it when you're near each other?"

"You have to be really close for that," I said, wondering just how close you had to be before you felt that tingling. *Or was it because I was a* vegan? I hadn't felt Joe when he approached me on the roof. *Why was that?* "And I can wear a disguise, so they won't recognize me."

Christian was shaking his head, but he said, "And where am I supposed to be while you are off playing spy?"

"In the parking lot. The license plates might tell us who's there and, depending on how it goes, I might need a fast getaway."

"Oh, I have absolutely no doubt that you'll need that when this ridiculous plan inevitably goes south. Maybe I'll get lucky and you'll all just take each other out."

Chapter 21

The Plantation was a roadhouse and casino located on the outskirts of Hammond, Indiana. The place was designed to look like a plantation of the Old South, with columns along the front portico and magnolia trees planted everywhere. It seemed to stick out like a sore thumb in northern Indiana.

We'd arrived in the late afternoon and I'd gone inside to start our plan. There was a dining area in the front and a casino toward the back. There were some private rooms and a large ballroom that was being set up for a fancy dinner. Some of Capone's men—I recognized them from the Lexington; thankfully, they didn't recognize me—were around already providing protection. That confirmed that something was going on.

I wandered toward the kitchen, which was in the basement. The place was busy with cooks and assistants dealing with the few customers that were here for an early dinner, but they also appeared to be getting ready for the banquet. I spotted a waiter who was carrying linens to another stairway that led to the ballroom that Capone would be using.

I followed the waiter—he was about my height and weight—into the stairwell. Nobody else was there and we were out of sight from the kitchen.

"Hey," I called. The waiter stopped on the landing

and looked at me.

"You're not supposed to be here," he muttered. "Staff only."

I moved quickly to the landing, almost appearing out of thin air right in front of him. His eyes widened, and I stared hard into them.

"Give me those," I ordered. The command was quiet, almost casual, and the waiter handed me the stack of linens.

"Take off your clothes," I commanded next. Without hesitation, he started pulling off his jacket. As he undressed, I set the linens down and started undressing as well. As he finished pulling off the shirt, I took it and put it on. When he stood there in his undergarments, I pointed to my clothes and said, "Put those on."

He complied and soon we stood there, him wearing my chinos, shirt, vest, tie, and jacket while I had on his waiter's uniform. "You're not feeling well," I said. "Go home. I'll take over."

He nodded, and I could see his face pale and a bit of sweat beaded on his forehead, like he really had a fever. I wondered how far my *vegan* powers of persuasion went, and if they were also less than what a full vampire could do. The waiter headed back down the stairs and I watched him head out of the kitchen.

That poor boy, Mom fretted, *He just can't resist you, can he? Just like you couldn't resist that red-headed harpy.*

It's not the same thing! I retorted, then picked up the linens and headed upstairs.

The ballroom wasn't large; it was really rather small, and it might have seemed intimate except for the thick green and gold curtains—along with the dark green wallpaper—that made the room feel claustrophobic.

A long table was being laid out in the middle of the room. Actually, it was three tables laid end-to-end. Two other waiters were placing a tablecloth over the tables.

"Hey, you're not Jimmy," one of them said as he adjusted his glasses. He was probably in his thirties, with short hair that was graying a bit and he had a thin mustache and beard. I looked at him, meeting his eyes.

"Jimmy's sick. I'm taking his place."

The man's face scrunched into a frown and I thought that my suggestion hadn't worked. But then he said, "Damn it, of all the nights to get sick. Fine, you know what the hell you're doing?"

"Yeah." He grunted and went back to placing the tablecloth.

Over the next couple of hours, Zachry (the head waiter), Kirt (the other waiter), and I got the ballroom set up for Capone's dinner. Place settings were laid out using good china and silverware, along with stemmed water and wine glasses. I thought I did a good job, though Zachry went behind me, fixing the placement of my forks, knives, and spoons and grumbling something about transient workers.

By around seven o'clock, everything was ready and Zachry allowed us a break. Kirt and I went to the stairs, Kirt pulling out a cigarette. I was about to ask for one when I caught a whiff of a distinctive hair pomade. I stole a glance toward the entrance to the ballroom just in time to see Frank Nitti walk in. I managed to step out of sight before he saw me.

"Mr. Nitti," Zachry said. "A pleasure as always."

"Everything looks great," Nitti said. "Wonderful. Our guests will begin arriving soon. Let's check on the dinner preparations. Mr. Capone wants everything to be perfect for tonight."

I could hear them walking toward me and I flew down the stairs. Nitti would certainly recognize me and I couldn't let that happen. I moved quickly toward the linen closet and stepped inside, pulling the door until it almost closed. Through the thin crack, I could clearly hear Nitti and Zachry come downstairs.

"What about the drinks?" asked Nitti.

"The bottles you sent over are stored upstairs in one of the side rooms. Are you sure you don't want us to store the wine in the cooler so it will chill for dinner?"

"No," Nitti said, and I could detect the slightest laugh in the word. "It's a special vintage of Mr. Capone's from Sicily and shouldn't be chilled."

Their voices increased in volume as they got nearer, and I stood as silently as I could in the closet. Since I had died, I found it odd that my body still did things as though I was still alive, like my heart still beat (though much slower) and I still breathed. I didn't know if it was an automatic thing, the body doing what it had always done, or a natural part of being a vampire. *More questions that I don't have answers to.* However, I had learned that I could stop these things if I tried; I could stop breathing without any ill effects, other than being unable to speak. I once stood that way, without breathing, for over four hours. I'd only stopped because I'd gotten bored.

I did that now, standing as silent as a statue as Nitti and Zachry toured the kitchen and inspected the meal being prepared. They passed the linen closet without opening it and, after a few minutes, I could hear them across the kitchen. Their voices were conversational, which for normal people would have been lost in the noise and clatter of the kitchen.

"May I use your phone?" asked Nitti.

"Of course."

I heard the phone call being made. I struggled to hear what Nitti said, or who he was talking to, but I couldn't make out the words. Suddenly I heard Zachry call out, "Five minute break everybody! Now!"

I was suddenly worried as this seemed very unusual. A memory of Mom's voice exploded in my head, *"Get back in the kitchen, Saul. You want to burn our apartment down by leaving the stove unattended?"* The admonishment had been when I was ten years old and I was supposed to keep an eye on the soup that she'd been making while she'd gone to answer the door. I'd gotten bored—I was ten, after all—and she'd scolded me the instant I'd stepped out of the kitchen without ever turning away from her conversation with Mrs. Cornisky.

I could smell food still cooking, but the clatter and noise of the kitchen had died. I was afraid, and I thought about making a run for it, but I could still hear Nitti chatting softly at the kitchen entrance.

Before I could decide what I should do, I felt a very familiar tingling sensation prickling up my spine. The doors to the linen closet were yanked open to reveal Al Capone. "Mr. Imbierowicz, what a surprise to find you here."

Chapter 22

The sudden shock caused me to take a step back and let out a gasp. Capone was wearing a dark suit with a crisp, sky blue silk shirt and a red and gold-striped tie knotted around his thick neck. A dark red handkerchief was folded into the pocket of his suit jacket and a black, snap-brimmed fedora with a red band was perched on his head.

Frank Nitti was walking up behind Capone, giving me a cruel, knowing smile. "He's not on the guest list." His hands moved to the inside of his jacket, getting ready to pull a gun, I was sure.

Capone stared at me and I did my best to avoid his eyes, but I could see the barest of scowls crease his face. "No," Capone said, in almost a whisper. Nitti pulled his hand out of his jacket without a gun in it. "Mr. Imbierowicz's tenacity is starting to grow on me."

I swallowed. It sounded like a compliment, but the statement had me worried. Capone smiled at me, looking like he was about to be photographed for the morning papers. "Let's go up to my room, Saul. I can't have one of my guests coming to dinner dressed like one of the help."

Capone stepped aside, gesturing with a wave of his arm for me to exit the closet. I walked out without hesitation.

Dad chided me. *What, now you trust this* shlang*? Did I raise a* shmegege*?* I didn't bother trying to answer as I didn't want to get into an argument.

"Excellent," smiled Capone. He turned toward Nitti. "Frank, see to the change of dinner plans and get Saul some appropriate attire."

If Nitti was angered or upset by Capone's decision, he didn't show it. With a nod, he headed out of the kitchen where I could see him in conversation with Zachry.

Capone led me out of the kitchen and toward a service elevator down one of the hallways. If I had any thoughts about making a run for it, that option was no longer available. But I didn't want to run. I didn't think I would ever be in a better position to try to find out what was going on.

The elevator was waiting for us, and Capone and I stepped inside the small space. I was distinctly aware of Capone's cologne, and the scar on his face had never seemed so prominent to me before. I wondered if he'd gotten the scar before becoming a vampire, as it should have healed completely if it had happened after he died. I'm sure I wasn't the first person to wonder where Scarface had gotten his distinctive feature.

"I am not surprised by you being here, Mr. Imbierowicz." Capone closed the doors of the elevator himself, pulling the lever that started lifting the car. "You were so desperate at my office that I knew you'd find a way to be here."

I bridled a bit at the comment. *I hadn't been desperate.* "The only thing I'm desperate to do is to put you behind bars and stop a bloodbath."

Capone gave a soft chuckle. "You can't stop me, and neither can that *idiota*, Ness. I own Chicago, and nobody can touch me here." He pulled the lever, stopping the elevator.

"We aren't in Chicago right now."

"Heh, a comedian." Capone turned to look at me. "You won't be making many jokes later on, Saul. Soon you will be one of us and you won't care what happens or want to stop me." He opened the elevator doors and stepped out into a narrow hallway on The Plantation's second floor. He led me down the hall and opened a nondescript door, gesturing for me to enter. I stepped into a small sitting room. There was a couch, a chair in front of a table and mirror, and a wardrobe. The room was decorated in soft green and pink colors.

"Please wait here, Mr. Imbierowicz. Frank will bring you a change of clothes and then we'll head down to dinner when all of my guests have arrived."

Capone left without another word, closing the door. I heard the sound of a key, then the click of the lock.

What a brilliant plan! I never would have thought that you'd want to become the prisoner of the man that you're trying to stop. You've got him right where you want him.

Shut up, Sarah.

Chapter 23

I sat down on the couch, thinking that, while this wasn't exactly what I had planned, it was still what I had wanted. I was with Capone. Now I just needed to learn who this other vampire was that was threatening him. Simple.

And what's your venderlekh *idea to do that?* Dad asked. *How will you learn Capone's secrets while keeping that monster from making you just like him?*

I didn't have an answer to that, so I stayed quiet. I knew that if I really wanted to break out of this room, I could. The door was flimsy, and the lock was cheaper than the one on my old apartment, but Capone had to know that, too, so it was better to stay put. I tried to think of a way that I could get Capone to talk about the other vampire. He hadn't acknowledged that there was a threat, except for showing a bit of surprise about the Chinese vampire. What did Capone have planned for his dinner? How did Capone plan on making me one of his thugs in a room full of dinner guests?

Why are you doing this? It was Mom this time. *The last time you almost drank poor Mr. Stafford's blood, and this time will be different how?*

I was tired and hungry last time, I tried to explain. *And I didn't want to become a monster.*

Yes, you did, Dad scolded. *You did want it. You would*

have bitten Mr. Stafford and become a monster just like him.

I thought we raised you better than this, Mom sobbed. *Certainly, if that's what you want to do then who are we to stop you? I suppose I can accept it if you want to become a monster.*

But I don't want to be a monster!

You have a modne *way of showing it,* Dad replied. *If you walk into the lion's den and expect to come out alive, you're wrong. All you'll do is break your mother's heart. Why don't you just get out now?*

I can't do that, I protested. *I have a job to do.*

Feh, Dad said dismissively. *What sort of a job is it? You lie to your co-workers. Your partner hates you. I would never have been a success at the packing plant if I lied or if my co-workers hated me.*

I'm not cutting up carcasses on the killing floor.

Oh, you think this is different? My son, who has— what—two months of job experience, thinks that I don't know what I'm talking about?

Listen to your father, Saul, Mom said. *He made supervisor, remember.*

This is different.

No. It's no different, Dad chided. *Why do you think you should do all of this for people who don't care about you?*

You should have gone with Joe, added Mom. *He's such a nice boy. Why did you never bring him home to meet us? Did we embarrass you?*

Of course he was embarrassed, Sarah chimed in. *He only ever had one friend. What would have happened if we didn't like him?*

Don't you get it, I said in exasperation. *This is bigger than just me, or what I want. Other people, innocent people, may get hurt. You always told me that I should help others and not think about myself.*

That seemed to shut everyone up. They'd always go silent whenever I threw one of their comments or suggestions back at them.

We just want you to be safe, dear, Mom finally said.

I'm not planning on doing anything stupid.

You never do, Sarah added. *But it just seems to work out that way.*

There was a snort from Dad, but no comment. Finally, he said, *So, what's your plan? It's not like this Capone fellow will just tell you what you want to hear.*

I didn't respond because I didn't have a good idea for finding out. *Some kind of super G-man I've turned out to be.*

You can say that again, Sarah quipped.

The sound of a key in the lock shook me out of my thoughts before I could figure out a plan. Frank Nitti stood in the doorway holding a bunch of clothes. He tossed them at me. "Put them on. The boss expects his guests to be *presentable*." He left without another word and I could hear the key turning in the lock again.

I separated the clothes, finding black slacks, a white shirt and bow tie, and a black dinner jacket. With a sigh, I started taking off my clothes.

As I was changing into my donated clothes, I heard a muffled voice, but one that clearly belonged to Nitti. "Telegram for you, boss."

I looked around, wondering where the voice was coming from. I didn't see anything until I looked up. High on the room's left wall was a metal grate. It was there to help circulate air between rooms and it must have been connected to Capone's room.

"It can wait," I heard Capone say. It was muted enough that a normal person might have only heard mumbling, if anything at all. To me, it was as if I was standing right there in the room with Capone. He must not have been aware that the grate was there, and I smiled at my good fortune.

"It's from Mr. Brown."

My ears perked up at the name. *It can't be the same guy,* I thought. *There's no way a man named Brown would go around wearing all brown.* I heard the envelope being opened, then silence, as I assumed that Capone was reading the telegram.

"Who does this *coglione* think he is!" Capone burst out. I think even Christian could have heard him from his post in the car.

"This piece of shit is demanding to meet in Atlantic City to give me an ultimatum. Can you believe the balls of this *stronzo*? Trying to give *me* orders!"

"Sounds like Mr. Brown's boss is getting too big for his own good," Nitti said sagely. I had to assume that it was an attempt to keep Capone's temper under control.

"Our mysterious adversary is definitely becoming a tiresome thorn in my side," Capone said.

I knew it! He doesn't know who it is.

Yes, yes, you're very smart, Dad said.

Especially for a guy whose whole plan was to get trapped in a hotel room, Sarah added.

Will you be quiet? I'm trying to listen.

Capone had apparently calmed down. "Trying to bring in a chink vampire is a serious threat. They knew I would have to respond to such an act."

"Did the *vegan* really kill it?" Nitti asked.

Capone's dismissive laugh was answer enough. I hadn't expected him to believe my lie.

"So, if they were there to meet the vampire, why'd they kill it?" Nitti asked.

"I don't know," admitted Capone. I could picture his brow furrowed in thought. "That's not important right now. Don't forget that our *special* guests tonight were being lured to the other side. My opponent is getting bold, and I aim to make him pay for it."

There was silence, but I figured that Nitti was nodding his head in agreement like the good lackey that he was.

"That will start tonight," said Capone. "But I think we should set up a meeting with Mr. Brown in Atlantic City. Getting rid of him will send a very strong message that *nobody* fucks with Al Capone."

Chapter 24

I finished getting dressed as I went over all of the information I'd just learned. Capone was being pushed by another competitor who was trying to take over. Apparently, the same Mr. Brown who had tried to kill me at the garage after the St. Valentine's Day Massacre, and who had saved Christian and me from the *jiangshi* the other night, was working for this person.

Capone hadn't mentioned the name of his mysterious opponent. I suppose it was possible that Capone's opponent was trying to remain anonymous, although I didn't understand why. *Maybe it's a vampire thing.*

Now all I needed to do was get through dinner without being tempted to become one of Capone's minions. I wouldn't learn what I still needed to tonight, and I had to let Christian know what I had learned. *I should make a run for it*, I told myself.

And what about Capone's guests? Dad asked. *The ones lured to the other side. Aren't they of any use?*

How? They won't admit to that, not in front of Capone.

Sure, run away then. Throw away any chance to learn anything important. You certainly know what you're doing after two months on the job.

Don't be so hard on him, Mom said. *If he wants to run, let him run. At least that way he'll be safe.*

Have you seen him run? Sarah asked. *There's no guar-*

antee that he'll be safe doing that, either.

I shook my head. *Fine. Maybe I can learn something else tonight.*

I finished putting on the dinner clothes. The pants were tight in the waist, though they flared along my thighs. The shirt and jacket were also tight, and narrow in the shoulders, but the sleeves covered my hands. *Who the hell did Nitti get this from, Charlie Chaplin?*

Thankfully, the bow tie was a Spur tie, so I didn't have to struggle with it. Learning to tie a bow tie was not a skill that a young Jewish boy ever needed to learn, and certainly not for the son of a packing plant worker.

Supervisor, Mom corrected me. *Your father worked very hard to get that promotion, so don't you go making light of it.*

I waited about ten minutes after getting the suit on before the door opened again. Frank Nitti stood there, wearing a nice, and well-fitting, dinner jacket. He'd applied fresh pomade to his hair. Standing behind him was Capone, wearing a pure white suit and jacket, with a pale green bow tie. Two large diamond rings adorned his hands.

Nitti stepped aside, and I walked into the hallway. "Are you ready for dinner, Mr. Imbierowicz?" Capone looked at my ill-fitting outfit and gave a look toward Nitti that might have been disgust or approval. Capone curled up the corner of his mouth in a half-smirk, so I finally settled on approval.

We walked to the elevator, Nitti in the lead, and took it down to the main floor. Lively sounds were coming from the casino, but I spotted a couple of Capone's goons standing watch in the hallway, apparently posted there to keep any unwanted guests away.

We entered the banquet room, and there were about ten or twelve other men already inside, gathered in small groups and talking amiably. Most of them were smoking cigars or cigarettes and nearly all of them held a glass tumbler filled with whiskey. Everybody was dressed in their best dinner suits and I saw the glint of many diamonds sparkling from their fingers.

When Capone entered the room, all conversation stopped, and applause broke out. Capone let it go on for a few moments before holding up his hands.

"Gentlemen, you do me honor by being here, but let us remember that we are here to honor others, not just me." He gave a wide grin and the guests all laughed at Capone's little joke.

A waiter appeared with a silver tray that had three drinks on it, holding it up for Capone, who picked up one of the glasses. Nitti did the same, and I took the last glass when the waiter floated the tray before me. Capone was the host, so everybody paid attention to him, but I could feel that many of the eyes had turned to ogle me as well. I felt self-conscious in my ill-fitting suit. I hadn't felt like I was under this kind of scrutiny since my *bar mitzvah*.

And we all know how that turned out, Sarah commented. I ignored her.

But what made my skin crawl and sent pinpricks of fear up my spine was the tingling sensation that I felt. *Vampires.* Besides Capone and myself, there were also other vampires in the room. I hadn't noticed it at first because of Capone—his presence had initially masked their own—but now I could feel them all; there was a strong prickling sensation on my neck, and the hairs on my arms began tingling. I couldn't tell how many of the others were vampires—maybe one, maybe everybody—my senses were not that attuned to this ability. *Is it an ability? Is this something that vampires can do, or is this because I'm a* vegan *with some vestiges of my humanity still inside me? One more question I probably won't get the answer to.*

Capone was moving among the guests, greeting each of them with a smile, some short conversation, and a pat on the back or shoulder. Nitti hovered near me, but he looked like he wanted to mingle as well.

"I don't need a babysitter," I said. "Do you think your boss or his vampire friends would let me out alive if I tried?" I lifted the drink to my lips to try to seem confident.

Nitti smiled, as if realizing that I was no threat to Capone, much less to anyone else, right now. He turned and walked into the crowd.

I sipped the whiskey and had to stifle a cough. I'd sampled a lot of the crap that passed for alcohol these days, but this was the real stuff, and I hadn't expected its strong flavor. Standing near the doorway, I didn't attempt to mingle or try to start a conversation. Some of the faces looked vaguely familiar, maybe from a newspaper photo, but I didn't know anybody's name.

People continued to stare at me. *Can they tell that I'm a* vegan? *What is Capone telling them about me?* I tried to listen in on the conversations, but there were so many of them going on that I kept getting distracted. All I could hear was a low murmur and snatches of words from a dozen people talking at once. I managed to calm myself and focus on just Capone, but all I heard were simple platitudes and chit-chat.

One of the guests walked toward me. At first, I

thought he was getting a refill, as I'd been hovering near the waiters, but instead he headed directly toward me. He had a slightly puffy face with sunken eyes and dark black hair that was cut short and had a slight widow's peak. I vaguely recognized his face from some newspaper story a few years earlier, but his name escaped me.

He held out his hand in introduction, and said, "John Scalise." He had a strong Sicilian accent.

I shook his hand and said, "Stan Kowalski," giving him my pseudonym.

"When did Capone start hiring Jews?" he asked.

"I don't work for him," I answered. "I'm here as a guest."

Scalise raised one thick eyebrow, and then nodded slowly. "You must be the one they're interested in," he said very softly. He studied me closely, trying to gauge my reaction.

I must have disappointed him because all I said was, "Who?" He started to turn away from me, "Who's interested in me?" I persisted.

Scalise turned back to face me, a look of incomprehension on his face. He started to say something, but was interrupted by Capone, who'd practically materialized out of thin air next to us.

"Come, John, you don't want to hang around a *vegan* like this," Capone gave me a look of pure disgust. "This dinner is in your and Albert's honor. Let's not ruin the evening by mingling with low-life scum."

Scalise nodded and let Capone lead him away from me, though he did give me a parting look that was filled with... disappointment, sadness, resignation? I really couldn't tell. *What had he meant by I'm the one they're interested in? Who are they? Who's interested in me?*

My mind went back to the warehouse in Chinatown. As the *jiangshi* was choking me to death, Mr. Brown had appeared out of nowhere and killed the creature, saving my life. *What was it that he had said? "She'll be happy to know you're doing well."*

Who was he referring to? Was it Mr. Brown's boss, or somebody else?

A new thought came to me as I sipped the whiskey and watched the gangsters mingle. Capone and Nitti had implied that Mr. Brown—if it is the same vampire—was working for whoever is trying to take over Capone's turf. *Does this mean that the vampire threatening Capone is a woman?*

An old memory, from my first encounter with Mr. Brown, came to me. As I had lain on the ground, catching my breath after Mr. Brown had tried to strangle me, he had said, "What is she playing at?" It hadn't made any sense at the time, but now it did. He'd been referring to his boss; some mysterious vampiress.

But why would she be interested in me? I've never met any female vampires.

No, that's not true, Dad said. *There was that Irish* kurva *you were dating who turned out to be a bloodsucking monster.*

Moira Kelly. *She's not a* kurva, *Dad.*

It's a good thing you never brought that girl home, Mom added. *What would the neighbors think?*

I knew it couldn't be her. I'd killed Moira, shoving a wooden chair leg through her heart.

So, who is Mr. Brown working for and why is she interested in you, of all people? Sarah asked.

I don't have the slightest idea, I admitted. But, for the first time, I actually knew something that Capone didn't. That realization made me smile as I finished the whiskey.

Chapter 25

As I stood pondering this new insight, I saw Zachry enter the room from the stairs. The head waiter gave a nod toward Nitti, who touched Capone's arm. "Gentlemen," Capone announced. "Let's eat."

The men all moved to the tables and took their seats. It didn't look like there was any assigned seating as everybody just picked a place close to them, or close to a friend. John Scalise took a seat on the opposite side of the room, whispering with another vampire who I assumed was Albert.

I paused, as I wasn't sure where to sit. Then I saw Capone gesture to the seat on his left. It was empty, with Nitti taking the next place over. Since I was Capone's "guest" he apparently wanted to keep me close. I took my seat, wondering how I might use my newfound knowledge to my advantage.

"I hope you are enjoying yourself, Mr. Imbierowicz." Capone was jovial, smiling as he held up a glass that was promptly filled with a dark red liquid.

"I've never been to a monster party before. Are they always this boring?" The waiter leaned between Capone and me, filling my glass.

Capone gave me a wry smile. "You may jest, Saul, but the night is still young." He took a drink of the thick red liquid and looked pointedly at my glass. I picked it up hesitantly, but I didn't get the scent of blood, just a well-aged wine.

"A Sicilian vintage," Capone offered. "Brought in before Prohibition."

I took a drink and nodded. I have to admit that since becoming a vampire—or *vegan*, or whatever—my taste in wines had improved. The wine I drank at my *bar mitzvah* had tasted too sweet and bitter. Now I could taste all of the subtle flavors that wine connoisseurs always raved about. I enjoyed the complex flavors that I found now in my mouth, and then swallowed. "It's very good," I acknowledged.

Capone accepted my compliment as several waiters glided into the room, each of them carrying two plates. They deftly placed the meals before each of the diners. Each plate was filled with a small chicken breast over pasta with a white sauce and a side of vegetables. More wine was served with the meal.

Conversation during the meal was light and focused on anything but Capone's business or whatever else it was that gangsters talked about when they gathered together. I don't know if this was normal, or if it was just because I was there. I was sure that Capone had told everybody here that I was a Fed working with Eliot Ness. They talked about boxing, dames, movies, and even the weather. As soon as that happened, I was positive that they were doing so due to my presence.

After the main course was finished, dessert was served: cannoli and pineapple upside-down cake, as well as coffee. Capone had been mostly silent during the meal, letting the others talk, and only joining in to laugh at a joke or acknowledge some point in the conversation. As the desserts were being finished, he signaled to

Zachry. With quiet efficiency, dessert plates, silverware, cups, and glasses were all removed and a tall, pewter goblet was set in front of each person. This must have been unexpected, as a few of the guests picked up their goblets in curiosity. Each goblet was etched with images of roses along the outside of the cup.

The waiters returned, each carrying a large clay bottle that was shaped like a bottle of Chianti. As they pulled the corks and began pouring a thick red liquid, I immediately knew what it was. Blood. The copper-iron smell hit me like a slap in the face. This wasn't cow's blood.

Saliva filled my mouth and my fangs grew longer. I could feel my pulse quickening in anticipation of my first sip. The red liquid was a mesmerizing pool in the grey cup and I had to force my attention away from it. I had to keep my mind focused on the room and what was going on around me. Everyone in the room, except for Nitti, had transformed, with large fangs protruding from lips, faces contorted into feral masks, and red glows shining in their eyes. I suddenly felt a tenuous connection to every vampire in the room, as if I was becoming part of their lives.

If feeding from a man that Capone had fed on would make me his servant, I thought, *what would drinking from this goblet of blood do?* This felt like an elaborate ritual; for what, I didn't know, but I knew that I couldn't drink the blood if I wanted to remain free of Capone's influence.

But the blood smelled so sweet, like the first smell from a freshly poured Coca-Cola, and I found myself licking my lips in anticipation. *I want it,* a voice mewed in my head and it took me a moment to realize that it was my own.

Doesn't it smell wonderful? Moira purred. *What are you afraid of? You're so close to becoming who you're meant to be. Why not just drink it and be done with it?*

Before I could answer, or talk myself out of it, Capone stood up. He lifted his goblet and what little conversation was going on ceased. Everybody looked at Capone.

"Gentlemen, I hope we have all enjoyed our wonderful dinner." There were nods of assent and murmurs from all corners of the room. Capone smiled, and it looked demonic as his lips moved around his fangs.

"I had originally wanted to give a little speech about baseball and teamwork, but I figure we're all too sophisticated for such a trite metaphor." Capone gave a little laugh and the others dutifully joined him.

"Instead, I thought this would be more appropriate." He held up his own goblet of blood. "This is a special... vintage," he chuckled softly, "that my mentor, Joe Torio, had kept for many years. He never had need to use it," a slight flash of red in Capone's eyes. *Anger?* "And he left it to me. It's called *Sangue del Servo Fedele* and came from a procurator who lived over 500 years ago and faithfully served his master his entire life. Drinking this ensures your loyalty to me. *Salut.*"

Capone raised his goblet and drank the blood greedily, letting some of it drip down the sides of his mouth. Others around the table were doing the same. I lifted the goblet and willed myself to not drink the blood, but the aroma, that beautiful fragrance, enthralled me and I found that I couldn't keep myself from putting the goblet to my lips.

The goblet tipped, the sweet blood rushing almost to my lips, when a commotion at the other end of the room drew my attention. John Scalise and Albert were flinging their goblets to the table, the blood spilling across the tablecloth, coating the white linen in a deep red sea. Scalise and Albert were trying to run, to escape the room, but the vampires around them were already reacting.

"Traitors!" Capone snarled, and he leapt from his chair, landing on the table. At the far end, vampires were throwing powerful punches at the two men. Scalise and Albert tried to fight back, managing to knock back a couple of their assailants, but they were quickly overwhelmed. Capone reached the end of the table and jumped down, throwing his own punches at the two vampires.

I recalled the pummeling that I had received at the hands of Capone back in February and flinched. I knew just how hard he could hit when he was angry. I set the goblet of blood back down on the table with a shaking hand; all my desire to drink it was now gone as I watched the two vampires being beaten at the far end of the table.

Capone was lost in the frenzy, his eyes glowing with an evil, reddish light, his face contorted. *Though it's not the same as how Joe had looked when he'd let me see his vampire form,* I noted. I'm sure that meant something, but I didn't have time to dwell on its significance. Capone threw a massive uppercut with his right arm, catching Scalise in the jaw. I saw teeth go flying.

Now's the only chance I'll get. I had been rooted to my seat, watching the brutal assault, but now I reacted. I stood up and turned to the door, passing Nitti, who had pulled a snub-nosed revolver and was walking toward the fray. He either didn't notice me or didn't care.

I made it through the door and started running hard down the hallway. As I reached the main entrance, I heard several gunshots coming from the banquet room. I slammed through the front doors and jumped down the six steps that led off the massive porch fronting The Plantation. My feet skidded on the gravel in the parking lot as I reached Christian's car. It was the same, beat-up Ford that he'd had back in February, but I was grateful to see that it was still parked here.

I yanked open the door, yelling, "Drive! Drive!" as I got in.

Christian had apparently been asleep, and he jerked awake with a start. "What...?" he asked in confusion.

"We need to go!" I yelled. "Now!"

"What happened?"

"No time to explain," I said, looking toward the entrance. I expected to see a horde of vampires bursting out of the main doors any second.

Christian finally understood my agitation and started the Ford. It looked like crap on the outside, but the engine started the first time. Christian pulled out and headed toward the highway.

I watched behind us for any sign of pursuit, but nobody seemed to be following us. As we crossed back into Illinois, I finally let out a sigh of relief.

Chapter 26

As we drove toward Chicago, Christian asked me, "What happened? Did you find out who's threatening Capone?"

"No," I said, letting my disappointment fill the single word. Christian let out a sound of exasperation, mixed with anger. I cut him off before he could say anything. "Let me tell you what happened before you call me incompetent again."

I proceeded to tell him what had happened, from my posing as the waiter, to Capone finding me, and the dinner. We were entering the south side of Chicago as I described the wild melee that had erupted at the end of the meal.

"They beat them to a bloody pulp," I said. "And I heard gunshots as I ran out, so I'm assuming they're both dead."

"My Lord and Savior," Christian murmured, and crossed himself, apparently not considering the fact that Scalise and Albert had been monsters themselves.

"I didn't want to stay around to find out what happened. The way they were all behaving, I think that I might have been their next target. Besides, I don't think Capone knows who it is that's threatening him."

Christian nodded. "You were lucky that Capone decided to put you on display for his underlings, otherwise you might not have heard about that telegram." Christian paused for a moment, navigating through the late-night traffic. "Do you think that was a setup? Did Capone know that you were listening to him?"

I considered this for a moment, finally shaking my head. "No. The grate between the rooms was high up on the wall. I didn't even notice it until I heard Capone's outburst, so no, I don't think that Capone knew about it."

We drove in silence for a few blocks. We turned, and I could see the sign for the Chicago Theater down the street. Christian pulled up in front of the theater, putting the car into neutral.

"So what do we do about tonight?" he asked.

I had given it some thought on the drive back. "Nothing," I said. "Even if we could convince the cops or a judge that Capone has personally killed two men, there's no way they'd believe how he did it. And it's not like I can reveal that I'm a vampire, either. Any sane person would either just laugh it off or throw me into an asylum."

"The Night Watchers would believe it," Christian said. I was a bit stunned, since he'd never brought them up in conversation on his own before. "But even though they'd believe us, I'm not high on their list of acceptable agents right now."

"Still in the doghouse after what happened in February?"

"You might say that," Christian admitted. "After Truesdale's plan to get Capone failed, I was pretty much kicked to the curb. I'm still an agent, but nobody wants anything to do with me. That's why I agreed to work for Ness."

I was floored. Christian had never opened up like this to me about anything before, let alone the mysterious Night Watchers. I wanted to say something, but I was afraid that, if I did, he'd just clam up again.

"If we can stop Capone on our own, that would be enough to get me back on the Director's good side."

"Then that's what we'll do," I said. "We know Capone is going to Atlantic City, so that's where we need to go."

Christian nodded. "But when is he going? It could be tomorrow, or next week, or even next month." He gave an exasperated sigh.

"We know." Christian gave me a funny look. "I mean Ness's team. Our team. We must know. We collect so much information from snitches and wiretaps, we have to already know."

"That means we're going to have to go to work tomorrow."

"Yep. Do you think Ness will be happy to see us?"

Chapter 27

"Where the hell have you two been?" Ness snapped. Christian and I were at our desks pretending to do paperwork. Ness still had on his hat and coat, the morning's paper tucked under one arm. He nodded to Christian, "And don't tell me that you were still 'ill' after the other night."

Christian looked like he was biting his tongue to keep from talking. "Can we tell you in your office?" I asked.

Ness glared at me, and the faces of Cloonan and Gardner, sitting at their own desks, looked disappointed. They were hoping to see a public tongue-lashing. Ness apparently understood my meaning and gave a curt nod before walking into his office. Christian and I got up and followed him.

Ness was hanging up his coat and hat as we walked in, the newspaper spread open on the desk. I closed the door as he turned to face us. "What the hell have you two been doing?"

Before Christian could say anything, I spoke up. "It was my idea," I said, and Christian gave me an appreciative glance. "After the incident at the warehouse, I learned some information about Capone and what might be going on."

"From who?"

"It doesn't matter," I said. Ness's look said that it did, but he stayed silent. "Another vampire is trying to force Capone out. They were the ones who brought in the Chinese vampire. There's a vampire gang war brewing, so I convinced Christian to help me see if we could find out what was going on so that we could put a stop to it."

Ness looked at Christian. "You agreed to help Saul?" He sounded surprised.

"Not at first," he admitted. "But he and I are the only ones on the team who know what Capone really is. We're the best ones to deal with him. It's why you wanted us in the group in the first place."

"I brought you on because I needed the manpower." He looked at Christian. "And you know better than to go out on your own without backup." He shook his head. "So did you find out anything useful? Something we can use against Capone?"

"Maybe," I said.

"Maybe?" Ness threw up his arms and sat heavily down at his desk. "I can't run an investigation on maybe."

"We didn't learn anything about who is threatening Capone," I said. "I am pretty sure that Capone doesn't even know. But I do know that Capone is going to meet with a vampire that's high in the other organization when he goes to Atlantic City."

"And how in the hell do you know Capone is going to Atlantic City?"

I tapped a small headline on the newspaper. It was under the fold but still made the front page, probably due to the gruesome nature of the murders. "Because I heard it straight from Capone himself, where *this* happened last night." I stabbed my finger at the paper.

Ness looked down at the headline.

Brutal Murder of Two Men
Bodies Dumped in Car in Hammond

"Capone did this?"

I nodded. "I was in the room. Capone—and about ten others—beat them to death. They were both vampires." Ness raised his eyebrows at that, "and they were also trying to defect to this other organization."

"Capone was sending a message," Christian added.

"Well, he certainly did that," Ness admitted. "Not that anybody will ever connect him to this."

"The one who matters to Capone will get the message," I said. "But nobody else will put it together. And even if regular folks could believe that Capone was capable of murder, nobody would buy that he did it with his bare hands." Ness gave me an appraising look, as if he thought that I'd never grow out of my "get Capone for murder" obsession.

"That's why we need to go to Atlantic City," Christian said. "If we can learn who Capone is meeting, we'll be able to stop a lot of bloodshed before it ever starts. Maybe we'll even learn something that will be useful in making a case against Capone."

"Capone is heading to Atlantic City in a couple of days," Ness said as he leaned back in his chair. "The rumors are that there's a big meeting of all the gang bosses: New York, St. Louis, Detroit. One of the rumors that we're hearing is that they are all going to tell Capone to cool his heels. The St. Valentine's Day Massacre brought down a lot of attention on everybody, and the other players don't like it."

"Capone won't like that at all," I said. "So how do we get there to find out what's going on?"

"We don't."

I felt my jaw drop open. Christian managed to keep his face impassive, but I could see in his eyes that he was just as flabbergasted as I was. "Why the hell not?" I asked.

"Because the orders came straight from the Director. We are not to interfere with any meetings between Capone and anybody in Atlantic City."

"But this could be a gold mine for us," I protested.

"We're building a good case against Capone and his allies here," Ness said.

"Taxes?" The word spat out with more contempt than I had intended. Ness gave me a hard look, though not directly into my eyes.

"Yes, taxes. We're never going to get Capone for anything violent or for violation of the Volstead Act. But the tax angle, which started from that ledger Capone was so interested in earlier this year—"

"And which caused so much trouble for me," I interrupted, giving an accusing look at Christian.

"—is going to be the best way to take down Capone," Ness continued, ignoring my remark. "It's not sexy," Ness admitted, "but it will be something he can't beat with force, and," he held up a finger to stress the point, "it will be something that his special status won't save him from. Everyone has to pay their taxes. Even the undead."

"So, while Capone is hobnobbing with gangster royalty in Atlantic City, what are we going to do?" I asked.

"We have some leads to work on. People we can interview and bank records to comb through. You'll stay busy."

"Oh, how fun," I let the sarcasm show. "Get the vampire to check the bank records because that's the best use of his impressive vampiric accounting powers."

"Get back to work," Ness said in dismissal. "Put any thoughts of Atlantic City out of your minds."

Christian nodded, but I hung my head in failure. We left the office, Christian closing the door behind us.

"I think we just blew our only chance of finding anything out," I grumbled.

Christian leaned over and whispered, "And I think we should check the train schedules to Atlantic City."

Chapter 28

Salty air filled my nose and I could taste the sea. Gulls hovered over the beach, riding on the wind currents. "It sure is different than walking along the shore of Lake Michigan," I commented.

Christian nodded, tipping his straw hat to two women walking the other way along the boardwalk. I belatedly did the same, giving the two ladies a glance.

"Christian, were you flirting with them?" I teased.

"What? No. Just being polite."

"And they were such pretty ladies to be polite to, too."

"I'm a devoted Christian, not a monk," he retorted. "I never took a vow of celibacy."

"Oh, do tell," I teased again. Christian's scowl could have curdled milk and he hurried his pace. "I guess it was a vow of silence, then."

Since suggesting we defy Ness's orders and take the train here to Atlantic City, Christian had opened up more to me, which meant that he didn't scowl at every word I uttered, or answer me in grunts and curses spoken under his breath. We weren't friends yet—I doubted that would ever happen—but he was at least starting to treat me like a partner. That was a huge improvement in my book.

I caught up to Christian. "I wish I could send my folks

a postcard. Mom always talked about visiting the beach with Dad someday, but they never did."

Silence hung between us for a few steps, and then Christian said, "It must be hard for you, not being able to see your parents."

I was stunned. Christian hadn't been this curious about me since before I had died. "It is," I admitted. "But it's weird, too. When I was growing up, all I wanted was to get away from them, to be on my own and to not have to live by their rules. The first chance I got, I moved out and into my own apartment. I found every excuse to not come over or to go to Temple with them." I kicked at some rocks, watching them scuttle along the board-walk. "Now I'd give anything to have just five minutes with them and tell them that I love them."

Christian remained silent and we continued our walk. After a few more minutes, we came to the President Hotel. It hadn't been hard to find out where Capone was staying. Christian had a contact in town who told him that "Nucky" Johnson had gotten all the gangsters rooms at the President. I had been able to confirm it by getting one of the guys at the registration desk to tell me. I had been surprised that Capone had actually reg-istered under his own name. So far, we hadn't been able to find out exactly where this meeting of the gangsters was taking place, or when, so Christian and I had been staking out the hotel in the hopes of spotting Capone or one of his men.

"See you in a few hours," Christian said. He moved around some tourists who were already out in a cou-ple of the ubiquitous rolling chairs that cluttered the boardwalk as he crossed and entered the hotel to keep watch from the inside. After the night at The Plantation, we'd decided that I should stay as far away from Capone as possible to keep him from knowing that I was here. It was really frustrating to have these abilities, but to also alert your presence like a lighthouse to any other vampires in the area. Not for the first time, I wondered if this was because I was a *vegan*, or if all vampires had this ability, but then I remembered my meeting with Joe on the roof. I hadn't felt his presence when he'd approached. *Why was that?*

I sighed as I walked over to the edge of the board-walk. *Yet another mystery that I'll probably never learn the truth about.* I was becoming resigned to never really knowing anything about what I had become.

I looked out toward the beach, and to the gray-green waters of the Atlantic Ocean beyond. It was early morning, but the beach was already filling with tourists. I walked along the boardwalk and took a seat on a bench. It had seats that faced both toward the ocean and toward the shops and hotels. I sat facing the buildings, with my back to the sea. Pulling out an unremarkable paperback book, I opened it up and began my surveillance.

The morning passed slowly. More tourists arrived to fill up the beach behind me. Other tourists and businessmen left the hotel, sometimes going for a short walk after breakfast or heading to wherever they were going. Occasionally, a taxi would stop out front to pick up a passenger with their luggage—probably heading to the train station—or a delivery truck would pull around the back of the hotel.

I hated this. It was more boring than sorting mail, if you can believe that. Ness and the others had tried to explain the importance of doing surveillance, but I didn't know how anybody wasn't driven insane by doing it.

And what, charging blindly into buildings has done you so much better? Dad asked.

Well, no, I admitted.

Maybe you should listen to people who have been doing this for more than two months.

I am listening, I whined. *I'm not running into the hotel am I?*

I could picture Dad giving me a noncommittal shrug. *Feh. So, for once in your life, you're finally listening to somebody. Will miracles never cease?*

This is boring enough without you nagging me.

Nagging? You consider me giving my son fatherly advice nagging? Feh! If you want nagging I can have your mother talk to you. Then you'll know from nagging.

What advice? I'm already doing what I should be doing.

But what else can *you be doing?* Dad asked patiently. *You have other skills, other abilities, don't you? Or is being a vampire all about just being stronger and faster than the other guy and sucking their blood?*

I paused to consider this. The meeting with the other gangsters had been planned in advance. They'd all know where to go and when to be there. Whatever they were meeting about it was just mundane stuff, at least as far as the gangsters were concerned; talking about territories and control, distribution of booze and drugs, and if Ness was right, taking Capone down a peg for letting Chicago get too bloody. Even in my two short months I had learned that too much attention to a gang was bad for business. That's what the gangs were: businesses that traded in illegal goods. The cops had stepped up enforcement in Chicago—a reaction after the massacre to show the fair citizens of the Windy City that they were doing something.

I laughed quietly to myself. *Maybe Ness is right and the best way to take down Capone and the others was by going after them for not paying taxes. Their income was earned from illegal activities so nobody paid any taxes on it. Why would they? It was crazy to do that.*

But that wasn't the whole reason why Capone was in Atlantic City. *He's also here to meet Mr. Brown,* I reminded myself. That meeting wouldn't be planned in advance. Mr. Brown and his boss were being cagey, tweaking Capone's nose by keeping him off-balance. Mr. Brown would have picked out a spot to have their meeting, but he'd want to make sure that it would be a surprise to Capone. Mr. Brown's boss would get a kick out of ordering Capone around, showing Capone who really had the power.

So how will this boss tell Capone where to meet? Dad asked.

Telegram. A messenger might be used, but it made more sense that they'd use a telegram. Mr. Brown wouldn't deliver the message in person himself for the same reason that I wouldn't go near Capone, and Capone might use his powers to compel a messenger to give up more information.

We should stake out the Western Union office, I suddenly realized.

But what if this Brown person has already sent his telegram? Dad asked.

It was a possibility, but I didn't think that was the case. I had no reason as to why, there was just something in my gut that told me that Mr. Brown would want to have his meeting later rather than sooner, either to keep Capone stewing for a while, or maybe to find the right place to have his meeting. Maybe both.

But we need to change our stakeout now, just to be safe.

Chapter 29

I closed my book and jogged across the boardwalk. It was a risk going inside, but I was willing to take it. I walked through the hotel's doors, nodding my head to the doorman who was standing watch. The lobby was mostly empty with the registration desk on my left and a collection of nice chairs, sofas, and coffee tables on my right. I spotted Christian, who was sitting in one of the chairs and reading a copy of *Life* magazine. He sat so that he could keep an eye on the two elevators at the back of the lobby, the registration desk, and the front doors.

He spotted me and I took off my hat and ran my hand through my hair. I then turned around and walked back outside. The doorman gave me a questioning look, but I ignored him and waited across the boardwalk.

Christian came outside a minute later. He gave me the same look that the doorman had given me and tried to ask a question, but I started walking down the boardwalk.

"What's wrong, Saul?" he asked, as he followed my brisk pace.

"We're watching the wrong place," I said.

"What? We know Capone is there."

"But we don't care where Capone is at now. We want to know where Capone will be meeting with Mr. Brown."

"Yes, but we don't know where he's staying," Christian countered, hammering home the points he had made on the train ride here.

"But he has to tell Capone where to meet," I explained, crossing the road and heading into town. "He won't do it in person, and I'm pretty sure he won't send a messenger."

"Western Union," Christian said, the light dawning for him.

"Exactly. If we stake out the Western Union office, we might be able to find out when and where Mr. Brown will arrange to meet with Capone."

"That's a good idea," Christian said, though he had a hesitant tone to his voice. "But surely Atlantic City has more than one Western Union office."

"Do you enjoy throwing cold holy water on everything?"

"I like to be prepared and not running off on wild hunches."

"You sound like my Dad," I muttered.

"What? Listen, watching Capone is a sure thing. We know he's staying there, and when he gets Brown's message, we can follow him to find out where they are going."

"And risk getting made in the process, or showing up after the fact. Look, I didn't say it was a great plan." We paused at a street corner to wait for traffic. "I think that Mr. Brown would use the telegraph office at the train station. So many people go through there that he'd be pretty anonymous in case Capone tried to track him before their meeting."

"I suppose that makes sense," Christian conceded, though he still sounded skeptical. As we headed across the road he asked, "What if Brown has already sent the telegram? What if he sends it from some other telegraph office? Or what if his master sends it?"

I shook my head. "Man, aren't you just full of sunshine?" We turned up the road toward the train station. "I'm guessing that Mr. Brown would wait until he got here before picking a location. And his master seems to give him a lot of leeway. Remember, he killed that *jiang-shi* when they'd been there to recruit it."

"I wonder why?" Christian mused.

"Haven't a clue," I said with a shake of my head. That question had been nagging in the back of my mind since Capone's dinner and I didn't want to discuss it now. "But it means that the chances are good that Mr. Brown will send the telegram from here after he's found the best spot for his meeting with Capone."

It took another twenty minutes of walking before we finally entered the train station. I wondered why Christian hadn't gotten his contact to loan us a car or something. I walked through the crowd of travelers who were heading into the city for a vacation on the beach, or to try their luck at the casinos, or rushing to catch their trains. We headed to the Western Union office and I walked inside. There were three windows where you could send a telegram, though at this time of the morning only one was open. I got into line behind a woman carrying a small suitcase and a hat box.

I only had to wait a few minutes and the teller called, "Next." He held out a hand for my telegram. I waited a beat for him to realize that I wasn't giving him anything and to look up at me. When he did, I made sure to look directly into his eyes.

"You need to help me," I commanded him.

"Sure, how can I help you?"

"My friend was supposed to send an important telegram to our boss, but he's got the wrong message, so I'm wondering if he sent it yet." *Ugh, that sounded really lame, even to me.*

"Look, bub..."

I cut him off with another command. "Check your log book. It's really important, and he's easy to remember. His last name is Brown, and he likes to dress all in brown clothes. I need you to tell me if he has been in." Another command at the end.

The teller looked through his logbook and shook his head. "No. No telegrams have been sent by a Mr. Brown."

"Thanks," I replied, and headed outside where Christian waited next to a newsstand. "Well, he hasn't sent any telegrams yet."

"From here."

I glared at my partner. "Were you always this cheerful with Truesdale?"

Christian chose to ignore my sarcasm, and said, "I guess we just have to hope that Mr. Brown will come here to send his telegram. That is, if he even decides to notify Capone with a telegram at all."

"Did you learn to be an eternal optimist as an altar boy, or were you always like this?"

"I don't like putting all our eggs in one basket."

"Go back to the hotel, then. I know this will get us what we need." I walked across the large hall and sat on a bench that let me see the telegraph office.

Christian paused for a moment, and then reluctantly sat down next to me. "I hope you're right."

"Are you telling me that you and Truesdale never played a hunch?"

"Only when we had no other options."

"Do you have a better option to find out where Capone and Brown will be meeting?"

It took a minute before Christian finally shook his head. "Not without getting made or showing up late and missing the whole thing."

"Trust me," I said. Christian snorted in response, and I tried to keep the million or so butterflies that had taken up residence in my stomach from showing.

Chapter 30

We sat on the bench for a couple of hours before Christian had to go relieve himself. He came back a while later with a paper-wrapped sandwich. One bonus of being undead was that I didn't have to take breaks either for the call of nature or to eat. Well, to eat real food anyway. I had brought some Thermoses filled with cow's blood with me since I didn't want to depend on finding someplace in Atlantic City to get blood. Christian had recoiled when he saw them—he knew exactly what they were for—and had muttered something about monsters under his breath. I'd clearly heard him—probably as he'd intended—but chose to ignore the comment. I figured I could go the rest of today before I needed to feed, but if Mr. Brown didn't show up soon, I'd need to go back to the hotel.

I was also nervous about confronting Mr. Brown and Capone. Even after feeding I wasn't a match for either of them alone, let alone if they decided to team up and work together to beat the crap out of me. Something about how Mr. Brown had acted around me previously suggested that might not happen, but I didn't want to take the chance.

Christian unfolded a newspaper that he'd also picked up and started reading. I continued to watch the Western Union office in the hope that Mr. Brown would come himself and not send some flunky.

"Did you hear that Carl Hubbell threw a no-hitter on the same day that those bodies were found?"

"Hmmm...?" Christian's question caught me off guard.

"I think the Giants might have a chance this year."

I turned to look at Christian. "What are you doing? For months you've wanted nothing to do with me. Now we're chatting about baseball like old chums?"

Christian folded the paper closed. "Don't mistake small talk for friendship. Two men sitting here and just staring at that office is suspicious. Two men chatting about baseball is not." He reopened the paper.

I grumbled to myself. *So much for thinking that Christian had turned over a new leaf.*

We spent the afternoon making "small talk" and watching the telegraph office. Around five o'clock, the station started to get busy as salesmen ran to catch trains and out of town visitors arrived. As more people entered the station, my clear line of sight to the telegraph office became obscured by people walking in front of me. In frustration, I stood up and pulled out my pack of Chesterfields. As I lit one with my Ronson, I moved through the crowd to get a better vantage point. I found a spot near a newsstand where I could see the office clearly.

I continued to watch as the commuters moved through the station. I was starting to doubt my plan, thinking that if Mr. Brown didn't show up, we'd never know when Capone met with him. They'd get away and we'd have lost any chance of learning anything about Mr. Brown's master. The butterflies had turned into bats and were swarming around my stomach now.

Then I saw him. At first it was just another brown fedora, like hundreds I had seen already today. I almost dismissed it as another false alarm when Mr. Brown stepped out of the crowd. He had on the same—or at least identical—slacks, jacket, shirt, and tie that I had seen him wearing before. That made him stand out a little bit, but the way he walked through the crowd confirmed his identity to me. He moved like a predator, how I'd imagined a shark would move through the ocean.

I watched him enter the telegraph office and I moved quickly back to where Christian was still sitting. "He's here," I said.

Christian gave me a look of stunned surprise. He hadn't thought that my plan would work. I wanted to be smug and tell him "I told you so" but I didn't want to lose Mr. Brown. I went back to watch the office.

Five minutes after he'd entered, Mr. Brown left the telegraph office, whistling softly to himself. I watched him head toward an exit with Christian following him. I waited and watched the office. A few minutes later, a messenger boy appeared carrying an envelope. I followed the boy as he headed outside. He crossed the road and headed toward the ocean. I waited until he was away from the station before moving to intercept him.

"Hey, kid, got the time?" I asked as I walked up behind him. The boy hesitated then turned to look at me. He started to speak but I locked my eyes onto his. "Let me see that telegram."

Now you're making a little boy go against his will? Mom scolded me. *What would Rabbi Gershwitz think?*

Yeah, who's the monster now? Sarah taunted.

This is important, I said, defensively. *Besides, he won't remember anything.*

And that makes it right? Dad asked, but they all kept quiet as the boy stopped and handed me the envelope. Neatly typed on the front was, "Al Capone, President Hotel." I smiled to myself.

The envelope had been only loosely closed and I was able to open it easily. Taking out the telegram, I read it quickly, then put it back in and handed the envelope back to the boy. "Hey, kid. You dropped this. You should be more careful."

The boy looked a bit stunned, and also embarrassed. "Thanks, Mister." He clutched the envelope with both hands and headed down the road. I turned and headed back to the station. Christian was waiting out front by the taxi stand.

"He got into a taxi," he said.

"Well, that's okay. I know where he's going to be tomorrow night at 9 o'clock."

Chapter 31

I closed the lid on the Thermos, setting it back into my suitcase. The cow's blood was starting to taste stale, but it hadn't gone bad yet. I was fully alert now; any traces of tiredness burned off like a morning fog. I needed to be at my best for this to work, and even then, I didn't think I could take on Capone and Mr. Brown alone.

I shut the door to my room and walked down the hall. I knocked on Christian's door. We were staying at a fleabag hotel well away from the boardwalk and the ocean view, but even so, the place still charged an arm and a leg for a room. Christian hadn't hesitated at the extra expense to make sure that he didn't have to share a room with a monster. He opened the door and stepped into the hall as he put on his hat. As we took the steps down to the lobby, I asked, "Are you nervous?" I had smelled what I took to be fear coming from him.

"A little bit," Christian admitted. "Going to face down two vampires isn't something any sane person would choose to do."

I nodded and put on my own hat as we reached the lobby. It was just after 7:30pm. We wanted to get to the meeting spot before the others did. The idea was that I'd find a position that was far enough away so that neither Capone nor Mr. Brown would notice my presence. Christian would get in closer and try to overhear their conversation.

† † †

The cab dropped us off at a deserted building well away from the bustle of the boardwalk. The building stood on the corner of Baltic and Connecticut Avenues, which was in a run-down part of town. "Nobody's going to make any money around here," I said.

Christian nodded his head in agreement.

The building we stood in front of looked like it might have been an old warehouse at one time, but colorful paintings of horses, elephants, and tigers on the walls and large lettering declared it to be "Gondorff's Carousel". The building sat on the corner, and part of the building had been cut at an angle with a ticket booth placed there. There were doors facing both streets, and a set of garage doors facing Connecticut. A sign was hung from the window of the ticket booth, stating that the carousel was "Closed for Repairs."

Christian and I had checked out the building that morning. We hadn't seen any workers and the doors had all been locked, with a large padlock on the garage doors. The building with the carousel was at least two stories tall. The building to the north was the same height, but luckily for us, the building to the west was only a single story. We'd investigated it earlier and knew that there was a row of windows along that wall that looked directly into the carousel.

Despite it being May, the weather was chilly, with a cool breeze coming in off the ocean. That was good, as it allowed us to wear our overcoats without too much suspicion. I'd spent the afternoon watching as Christian had loaded a silver cross, three vials of holy water, and a pair of wooden stakes into his coat. He'd also loaded a pistol with eight bullets, explaining that each bullet had been molded from silver.

I hadn't bothered to bring anything. I'd never fired a gun and, if we pulled this off, Capone and Mr. Brown would never even know that we'd been there.

We walked to the end of the street and found a fire escape. I jumped up and pulled the ladder down so that Christian and I could climb up to the roof and back toward the carousel. The windows were only a few feet higher than the roof that we stood on, and a couple of them were even open.

I walked over to one and pushed it open further, sticking my head inside. I could see the carousel sitting in the middle of the room; horses, swans, and other animals were staggered at different heights around the deck. There were some tables and chairs scattered around the edges of the room and in one corner was a cart for popping popcorn and another for roasting peanuts. The wall to my left had a set of stairs that led up to a balcony and a single door set in the wall.

"Well, the good news is that the place is empty," I said, as I pulled my head back out.

"And the bad news?"

"We're about eighteen feet off the ground and there's nothing under the windows on this side."

Christian stuck his head in and pulled it back. "Are you sure? It's as black as Satan's heart in there."

"Trust me." Christian looked at me, his eyes narrowed, then he nodded. "We could try the other building," I offered. "It looks like there's a door from that building that connects to the carousel."

Christian considered this, and then shook his head.

"Let's not waste the time. We can go in through here. Just lower me as far as you can and I'll jump." Without waiting for a reply, he crawled through the window, turning around to hang by his arms. Leaning in, I grabbed his wrist and lowered him as far as I could without falling.

"Okay," he said, and I let go. Christian dropped about eight feet to the floor. The sound of his landing echoed around the building. We both froze, waiting for somebody to shout or come running, but nobody did. Christian moved a few feet away and I jumped down after him, my landing softer, and considerably quieter, than Christian's had been.

Christian pulled out a flashlight and flicked it on, casting a beam of white light around the room. There was a small stack of crates sitting in front of the garage doors. He pointed the light at the two sets of entrance doors. "I doubt Mr. Brown and Capone will enter the same way we did. "

I nodded, and then realized that Christian couldn't see me in the dark. "If they are going to have a meeting anywhere, it will probably be between the entrance and the carousel. Unless they use sign language, I'll be able to hear them anywhere in here." I pointed toward the carts. "Those carts are as about as far away as I can get."

Christian shone the flashlight around, finally seeing the balcony. "What about up there?"

"There's a line of sight to there from the entrance. Even in the dark Mr. Brown or Capone will be able to see me. The carts will offer me some cover."

Christian nodded, apparently satisfied with my decision. "I think the carousel gives me the best place to hide." Without another word, he walked toward it.

With a shrug and a sigh, I walked toward the carts.

I could smell the oil, butter, salt, roasted peanuts, and burnt kernels as I approached; each odor sharp and distinct. *The smell will certainly mask my scent*, I thought. I got into position behind the carts. I saw Christian's light bob and trace a line around the carousel for a couple of minutes, then settle down and finally flick off. My eyes instantly adjusted to the total darkness and I could only spot Christian tucked in amongst the machinery of the carousel because I knew where to look.

Then we waited.

Chapter 32

The scrape of a key in a lock, then a door opening and closing, alerted me that somebody had arrived. The sound was louder than I expected in the mostly open space, loud enough that Christian should have heard it. I stole a glance at my wristwatch and saw that it was a quarter to nine. *Must be Mr. Brown,* I thought.

The carousel stood in the center of the room and blocked my view of the two entrances, but through the gaps between the wooden horses and swans I could see movement near the door that exited onto Baltic Avenue. I then heard the sound of a switch being thrown.

Lights spaced along the ceiling's rafters at the front of the building came feebly to life, slowly brightening as their filaments warmed up. I flinched, expecting the lights over me to also come on, but they stayed dark. I wondered why Mr. Brown would bother with turning on the lights at all since he and Capone could see just as well in the dark as I could.

Maybe he's setting the mood, Moira remarked.

I heard the sound of footsteps click across the wooden floorboards. Mr. Brown walked over to the other entrance and unlocked that door. He then walked toward the wall opposite me and I could see glimpses of him wearing his distinctive monochromatic wardrobe. He grabbed a table and two wooden chairs, easily picking all three up, then moved them toward the carousel.

I felt my muscles tighten in anticipation, expecting the tickling of my skin, but nothing happened. I was about sixty or seventy feet away from Mr. Brown and I tried to picture how far away I'd been from Capone and Brown each time I had felt the strange sensation. I think it had always been within about twenty feet, so I hoped that I was still hidden. Mr. Brown set the table and chairs down, arranging them slightly, and then sat down on one of the chairs. He hadn't reacted or shown any indication that he'd sensed my presence, or that he'd noticed Christian in his hiding spot, so I started to relax.

I knelt next to the popcorn cart so that I could get a clear view of Mr. Brown between the front legs of a rearing horse on the carousel. He took off his fedora and pulled out something from his coat pocket. A moment later, I heard the flick of a lighter. Bluish smoke wafted up from Mr. Brown and, a few seconds later, I could smell the cigar smoke even over the mixed odors coming from the carts.

By now the lights were fully lit, casting a yellowish glow along the front of the building. This created a long shadow from the carousel toward the back of the room. It would have been great if we'd been spying on regular humans, but it wouldn't do much good against creatures that could see just as well in the dark.

Mr. Brown sat quietly, slowly puffing on his cigar. I glanced at my watch every few seconds, my stomach doing slow somersaults as I watched the progression of the minute hand. Nine o'clock came, but Capone didn't show. Another minute went by, and then another, and I actually saw Mr. Brown check his own watch with a quick jerk of his left wrist.

At 9:05pm, by my watch, the door that faced Connecticut Avenue opened and shut with a soft click. I twisted to look under the peanut cart, and I watched Al Capone walk into the light. He wore a stylish, cream-colored summer suit with a matching vest. A sky-blue shirt collar circled his thick neck and he wore a tie of solid sapphire blue. He was flanked by two bodyguards, each wearing dark suits and overcoats. I couldn't tell from here, but they had to be vampires. The goons stayed by the door and Capone walked toward Mr. Brown, pulling off his white Panama. He stopped a few feet away from Mr. Brown, taking in the carousel.

"A bit melodramatic," he commented, finally fixing Mr. Brown with a look. His characteristic scar seemed to stand out on his face.

Mr. Brown shrugged, "We needed someplace public so we could get in, but neither of us wanted a crowd for this." He looked in the direction of the two goons. "I thought I instructed you to come alone. This is a private matter we are discussing."

Capone gave what I could only describe as a sheepish smile. He was trying for apologetic, but I don't think Capone had ever apologized for anything in his entire life. *Or his entire death, for that matter.* The smile looked odd on him and he must have known that it wasn't right because he let the smile fall after only a moment. "Nobody gives *me* orders, Mr. Brown."

I couldn't read Mr. Brown's reaction to that. After a moment, he held out his cigar case to Capone. Taking one, Capone neatly tore off one end and leaned over the table, allowing Mr. Brown to light it. Capone never took his eyes off of Mr. Brown the whole time.

Once the cigar was lit, Capone stood up. He took a deep pull and blew out a cloud of smoke. He didn't move to sit in the only available chair. "Now, let's get this over with," Capone said, with all pretenses of pleasantries gone, "I'm missing a party to humor you and your master."

I saw no visible reaction from Mr. Brown, so he probably recognized Capone's bluster for what it was. He blew out a thin stream of smoke before speaking, his voice low and steady. "You are under the impression, Mr. Capone, that this is a negotiation. It's not. My master sent me to give you a simple choice. Give us control of your organization and let your friends, those charming gang leaders that you've been meeting with the past couple of days, know that we are now in control of Chicago. If you don't, my master will take it from you through very public, and very bloody, force."

Capone pulled the cigar from his mouth and gave a sharp bark of laughter, edged with anger. "You tell your fuckin' master that he better crawl back into whatever shithole he crawled out from or I'll cut his fuckin' head from his fuckin' neck and stick it on my fuckin' wall. I don't know what made you think you could try to intimidate *me*, but *I* control Chicago. It's *my* town, and *nobody* messes with *me!*" He stuck the cigar back in his mouth, and smiled around it. "Or didn't the message we sent with Anselmi and Scalise sink into your master's dense skull?"

Mr. Brown's shoulders moved up and down ever so slightly, as if he was laughing quietly to himself. "You sent no message, except to confirm that you are a hot-headed wop who reacts the same way to every threat; by bashing it with your dumb, thick head." I could see Capone's neck redden at the insult. "But my master already knew that. All you did was drive more of our kind to my master. You are losing more and more control by the day, and you don't even know it. You've been losing your grip on power ever since you pulled that stunt on Valentine's Day."

Capone gave a malicious grin, recovering some of his anger. "So that's what this is about. Your boss is mad because I aborted some *vegans* before they could slither out and infect my city. Now he wants revenge?" Capone gave a slight chuckle, almost like a hiccup. "Well, your boss can go fuck himself. I'll kill him just like I did those fuckin' *vegans*. And maybe I'll send your boss another message, starting with you."

I gave a quick glance at the two goons and saw them reaching for the inside of their overcoats where, by the look of it, they were each carrying a Tommy Gun. Mr. Brown had also gone a bit red and I could see him clenching a fist under the table. I recalled that Mr. Brown had referred to the victims of the massacre as brothers, and I wondered if that had maybe been in the literal, as well as the figurative, sense. Mr. Brown seemed to also notice the two goons obviously going for their guns and he started to respond when he suddenly froze. In fact, everybody in the room froze, myself included. There had been a subtle click, too quiet for Christian to have heard, but clearly audible to me, Mr. Brown, Capone, and his two goons. Somebody had just unlatched the door that opened onto Baltic Avenue, and was trying to keep quiet. Capone's eyes narrowed and his forehead furrowed as he glared at Mr. Brown. For his part, Mr. Brown stayed quiet and shook his head once, stabbing a finger at Capone. Every vampire in the building turned to look at the entrance.

With a rush, the door was pulled open, and in charged two uniformed police officers. They each held shotguns at the ready, racking in rounds as they entered the building. Behind them entered a man wearing a light brown overcoat, a detective or other high-ranking cop. A dingy brown fedora covered his dark hair and he held a pistol. "Nobody moves!" The cop yelled. "You're all under arrest."

I recognized the voice and my stomach fell. Had I had any of my own blood left, I'm sure it would have run cold. Eliot Ness stepped into the light and raised his gun toward Al Capone.

Chapter 33

Shit. What the hell is Ness doing here?

As soon as Capone recognized Ness, his hand moved in a blur into his coat pocket, and pulled out a revolver. "If the master is here, that means the lapdog can't be far behind. Come out, come out, wherever you are, Mr. Imbierowicz."

The two cops seemed to be stunned by what had happened. I'm sure that, to their eyes, it had looked like Capone had just magically produced a gun from out of nowhere, like he was Harry Houdini. Capone turned in a fast circle, taking in the carousel and the rest of the room. His eyes narrowed slightly, and he fired his gun, the loud bark of the shot echoing around the room.

The bullet ricocheted off the side of the carousel and Christian scrambled from his hiding place. I took off from a sprinter's stance and ran all out, pushing my legs hard, my arms pumping, as I ran toward Capone and Mr. Brown. The gunshot seemed to have broken the spell as everybody now started to move and shoot.

I heard multiple gunshots coming from different parts of the room, followed by the loud boom of a shot-gun. Then there was the staccato sound of a Tommy Gun. Mr. Brown leaped high into the air to avoid the fusillade of bullets from one of Capone's goons. He did a flip and landed a few feet away from the cops and Ness, his face contorted into a demonic mask, his fangs long, sharp daggers that extended from his mouth.

Another spray of bullets flew toward the carousel, the rounds digging into the horses, elephants, and other circus animals. I could see Christian weaving through the animals, trying to escape the barrage. Capone took aim with his snub-nosed revolver and fired at Christian, the bullet taking off the ear of the tiger that Christian was hiding behind.

Too much was happening, and I felt powerless to do anything. I was fast, faster than any normal human, but the four full vampires were even faster. I felt like Gabby Hartnett trying to outrun Kiki Cuyler. I made a quick decision and ran toward Capone's goons. One turned toward me and pulled the trigger, but nothing happened. He'd already fired all of the rounds in his clip, and I was thankful that he didn't have the larger drum magazine on the submachine gun. In his surprise at being out of ammo, I was able to grab the gun, the barrel burning my skin, and ripped it out of his hands. I threw the weapon away as he threw a punch at me that landed square on the side of my head. I fell down in a heap, pain exploding in my mouth. Something hard rubbed against the inside of my mouth and I spat out a bloody tooth.

The other goon was bringing around his Tommy Gun, the barrel pointing at me. I expected the shot any moment, but at that instant, I managed to see Christian as he rose from behind the tiger and fired two quick shots from his pistol at Capone. The first one struck Capone in his shoulder, and he reacted in a blur, causing the second bullet to miss. Blood welled up from the spot where the first bullet had struck, and Capone yelled in pain. The two goons looked away from me and focused their attention on Christian.

Bullets from the Tommy Gun lanced across the room, shredding the tiger. Christian ducked away from the fire, but he wouldn't last long. I kicked out with my leg and struck the shooter in the knee. I was satisfied to hear a cracking sound as the knee shattered. I then climbed to my feet and ran toward Christian.

I saw Capone jump and he appeared to fly the twenty feet that separated him from Christian. He landed behind the tiger and Christian brandished the large silver crucifix he'd stashed in his coat. He stretched out his arm, trying to articulate some prayer, but Capone backhanded the cross, sending it clattering across the room. I could hear the loud snap of a broken bone.

Capone raised the revolver and pointed it at Christian. I had no time to think, or to come up with a strategy. I could see Christian stiffen in expectation of the gunshot.

You need to do something, or your friend's going to die! Dad exclaimed.

Not if I can help it!

I channeled every ounce of speed that I could muster, and launched myself toward Christian, hoping that I would be fast enough. The hammer struck home on the bullet, the soft bang of the shot sounding tender and quaint after the loud explosions from the Tommy Guns. Three more shots followed in rapid succession. I looked down to see four crimson flowers blossom on my chest as blood stained my shirt. I suddenly felt my legs grow weak and I fell to my knees. At the same time, there was a stinging sensation on my neck and I then heard Capone yelling.

"Fuck! You fuckin' piece of shit!" His voice was filled with rage and pain.

I looked up and saw Capone holding a hand to the side of his face, with what appeared to be steam curling around his fingers. His forehead was creased, ridges of skin pushing down on his eyes, his mouth open with long fangs protruding from his jaw. He started to lunge at us but his face and hand sizzled and smoked again. "May my blessed water cast out the hell-spawn before me!" Christian intoned, a bit melodramatically, I thought. More holy water splashed and the flesh on Capone's hand curled and bubbled where the water had struck.

Capone stumbled back and there was a blur of movement as the goon with the two good knees grabbed his master. Christian flung more holy water and the two creatures fled back toward the other door. I continued to hear gunfire coming from somewhere but couldn't tell where. Capone seemed to regain his composure and stood up, pulling his hand away from his face. His scar stood out like a bright red line now. One goon hobbled on one leg and held open the door, urging his master on. The gunshots were louder now.

"Another time, Mr. Imbierowicz," Capone called. He turned and ran outside, his coat flapping behind him like a cape.

I hadn't really been injured since I became a vampire, except for that time at the warehouse when Nitti had shot me. I had healed fairly quickly after that wound, but that had been just a single bullet that had grazed my shoulder. Now I had four bullets lodged inside my body. My heart continued to beat, but I grew lightheaded and tired as each beat seemed to leak blood faster than my body could heal.

Christian appeared in front of me, eyes wide and face showing a look of concern that I'd never seen from him before. "Saul, are you alright?"

What a narish *question,* I thought. *I was just shot!* "Oh yeah, I'm just peachy," I managed to say. My chest was on fire and I could taste blood in my throat as I spoke. I got up and Christian's eyes widened further.

"What are you doing, Saul? You need to stay down." He looked at my shirt, part of him wanting to help me, another part either unsure of what he could do, or too afraid to touch me.

"We've got to go after Capone," I said, trying to move. The room spun. *Who turned on the damn carousel? Wait, it's just me.*

"Capone's gone. And it sounds like Brown is chewing those cops to shreds."

I could hear screams and yells coming from the direction of Baltic Avenue. "Where's Ness?" I asked, blood seeping from my mouth.

"I don't know. I think he went outside to take on Brown."

That thought gave me new energy and I tried to walk forward but Christian placed a hand on my chest. "Don't move, Saul. Even when you weren't injured you couldn't have stopped Capone or Brown."

"I have to try. It's my fault that Ness is here."

"It was my idea to come to Atlantic City," Christian protested.

"Still, I'm the only one that has a chance against them. Ness will die if I don't help." I took a step, my legs shaking and numb. I couldn't feel my foot when I set it down and the room tilted wildly. Christian barely managed to keep me from falling.

He was silent for a moment. I took a breath, mostly in an effort to steel my resolve, since I didn't need the air for any other reason. I managed to take a couple of steps toward the entrance.

Christian appeared instantly (to my befuddled brain) in front of me, doing a really good impression of a vampire. Before I could say anything, he worked his good arm out of his overcoat and held his wrist out in front of me. "Feed on me."

Chapter 34

I stared at Christian, my mouth slack. I shook my head to clear it and tried to walk around him. He stepped back to stay in front of me, with his wrist still exposed.

"What are you doing?" I asked, my exhaustion magnifying the exasperation in my voice.

"You'll die if you try to take on Brown like this."

"I'm already dead," I shrugged. "And I'm not going to kill one partner to save another."

"*Putz*," Christian smirked. I was taken aback by him calling me a fool in Yiddish. "I don't want you to kill me." I looked at him, the confusion that I felt clearly showing on my face.

"You can feed on me and not kill me. I know you've refused to kill because you thought it would make you a monster, like Capone and Brown."

"Are you saying that by feeding, but not killing, I won't become a monster?" *Had Christian been hiding this information from me all along? Didn't Joe say something along those lines? My mind was too clouded to remember.*

"Oh, no. You'll still be a monster. You are already an abomination unto God." Christian gave me a slight smile. "But you won't be like Capone. You won't have killed." He held up his wrist again. "This is the only way we can save Ness."

"Why?" I couldn't help asking. "Ever since I showed up at your door with Ness you've hated me."

"That's not true. I've loathed you."

I tilted my head to acknowledge the fact, and nearly lost my balance. "Then why the change of heart?"

Christian pointed at my wounds. "You saved my life. You are willing to sacrifice yourself for me. For Ness. You may be an abomination in the eyes of our Lord, but maybe you aren't too much of a monster." He held up his wrist, shaking it slightly. "Now feed, before Brown has a chance to kill our boss."

I took his wrist in my hands and leaned down. My teeth rubbed against my lip as my fangs extended. A sweet, copper-rich smell reached my nostrils and I started to salivate.

Finally, Moria sighed. *Drink him dry. Take your power.*

Are you sure this is what you want? Mom asked.

Things will never be the same after this, Dad added.

You don't need to do this, Sarah pleaded.

I know what I'm doing! That elicited a "hmpf" from Dad. *It's the only way to save Ness.* I opened my mouth and placed my fangs on Christian's wrist. It took only the slightest pressure for me to puncture the skin.

The smell of his blood slammed into me, a powerful and aromatic scent. Then it was in my mouth and it tasted sweeter than the purest of honey. I swallowed the first drops, then more. It had a richer flavor than cow's blood, fuller bodied and almost electric in the sensation it gave me. As soon as I had tasted the first drop my senses came to life, like I'd really been dead for the past two months and I had just woken up.

I continued to feed, strength returning to my limbs. I was no longer standing shakily, and I could feel an influx of energy—life—coursing through my body. I felt the wounds on my skin, on my heart, and in my bones being healed. With each drop of blood that I consumed, I could feel my heart beating faster.

Christian's hand tried to pull away and I gripped it tighter, unwilling to give up on this bountiful meal.

Yes! That's it, Moria exhorted. *Keep going. You're almost there.*

His hands moved again, yanking against my mouth and a growl escaped from my throat. It was as if I'd never eaten a bite of food in my life. I was a starving man taking his first meal, a lost soul drinking from a clear pool after crossing a desert. The blood continued to flow.

Then I felt a sharp pain, a sting on my ear and cheek. It was an annoyance at first, and I tried to ignore it, to continue feeding. Then it quickly grew to be a hot, burning pain and I broke away from Christian's wrist, my eyes wide, and I snarled a guttural growl up at Christian.

Aw, Moira pouted. *You were so close.*

Christian held an empty bottle of holy water and took a wobbly step away from me. His face was pale, almost ashen, but he stared down at me. "Enough." His voice was breathy, tired. Drained.

My own face flushed, heat rising up my neck to my cheeks. "I'm sorry. Sorry." I stammered. I felt a drop of his blood on my lips and I greedily licked it up.

"Let's not do that ever again." He pulled out another vial of holy water from the inside folds of his coat and poured the liquid over the wound on his wrist. I was surprised to see it smoke a little. He took a few tentative steps and collapsed down in the chair that Capone had refused to use. "You go get Ness. I'm just going to catch my breath first."

"Are you sure? Your arm is broken." I gestured to his right arm. "And I nearly bled you dry," I added sheepishly. I wanted to stay, to make sure that Christian would be alright, but the sounds of gunfire, and the cries and screams coming from Baltic Avenue had died down.

"I'm fine," Christian managed to say, through gritted teeth, clearly in intense pain. "You go finish this."

I gave Christian one final look before I sprinted past the two dead cops by the door and rushed out into the night.

Chapter 35

All of my senses were on high alert as I left the carousel and the first thing that hit me was the smell of blood. This wasn't the fragrant, savory smell that had come from Christian's blood as I had fed. This was a cloying, offensive smell of blood mixed with sweat, fear, piss, and shit. The street looked like a bomb had gone off. The bodies of eight or nine or maybe even a dozen cops were strewn along the road. It was hard to tell because limbs had been torn from bodies and casually tossed aside.

I didn't have time to take in the scene in any great detail, or to see if Ness was among the dead. There was a blare from a horn and the sound of a crash—quite distinctive and loud in my ears—from my right. An older Model T Ford had driven up onto the curb and hit a telephone pole. Steam gushed from a damaged radiator. I might have taken it for a bad driver, or somebody so shocked at turning the corner into a bloodbath that they'd left the road, but the screech of tires from another car, turning left and heading toward the beach, told me that somebody was making a getaway.

Mr. Brown. I took off at a run, heading down Connecticut Avenue in pursuit. I gained speed, my legs pumping effortlessly. I felt as if I was as fast as the wind. I jogged to the right up another road, and then turned down an alley. I jumped a trash bin and the fence behind some tenement. I had never felt this alive—this *powerful*—before.

I could hear the sounds of horns blaring and tires squealing coming from the road. New Jersey Avenue, I thought. I turned in that direction and could see chaos on the road as cars had stopped in the middle of inter-sections or had turned roughly into curbs to get out of the path of a crazed driver. I could see the car a block ahead of me now, swerving around slower cars, its lights off.

I saw a flash of light come from the inside of the car, and it suddenly swerved to the left across oncom-ing traffic. The car hit the curb and bounced across the sidewalk, scattering a few late-night revelers. It came to a sudden stop as it crashed into an iron railing that sur-rounded the Breakers Hotel. People were approaching the car to see what had happened, or maybe to pummel the driver for causing such a mess. I continued to run, but before I could reach the crash, the people around the car scattered as the driver got out. It was Mr. Brown, and he was dragging Ness out of the car with one hand. In the other he held a Tommy Gun. The submachine gun was the cause for the sudden panic as people decided that it was safer to leave a gun-toting gangster alone.

Mr. Brown either didn't see me or didn't care about my presence. He grabbed a handful of Ness's coat and dragged him down the sidewalk toward the boardwalk. It looked like he was limping slightly and, as I reached the car, I could smell fresh blood.

The front end of the car was crushed. Glancing inside, I saw that blood had been smeared across the driver's seat, and a small pool of it was on the floorboards. Beneath the strong odor of blood, I could also smell the sharp metallic tang of gunpowder. Leaning in, I could see the grip of a pistol sticking out from under the passenger seat. I grabbed the gun and stuffed it into my coat pocket. The gun must have been in Ness's possession, and he'd managed to surprise Brown and gotten a lucky shot off.

Looking toward the boardwalk, I saw late-night strollers panicking and running up the street. Several rolling chairs had been tipped over and people were pulling friends, wives, and a few children away from the man waving the Tommy Gun. I ran toward him.

My feet made a rapid thumping on the boardwalk, fast enough that they almost sounded like the rapid fire from a machine gun. More people jumped out of my way with panicked screams. Gevalt, *I'm not the one with the gun, people*. Mr. Brown gave a quick glance behind him, and then pushed Ness toward a wide pier that poked out into the ocean. It had a small flower garden planted in the center behind a building, and I saw large signs advertising "Underwood Typewriter" and "The HOOVER Action Sweeper". Mr. Brown dragged Ness toward the garden, and I followed them.

Suddenly, Mr. Brown shoved Ness hard to the ground. He landed in what looked to be a large rose bush. Brown whipped around, and the Tommy Gun spat out lead and flame in a wild, uncontrolled arc. I heard more screams and running feet as I dove behind a hot dog cart. The bullets finally caught up with me and began chewing into the cart and wood around me, lukewarm hot dog water pouring onto the boardwalk.

I somersaulted forward behind a bench and another cart as the space where I'd just been was pelted by a dozen bullets. Mr. Brown was standing in the middle of the garden, Tommy Gun grasped in both hands, the gout of flame from the barrel illuminating his face and giving it a ghoulish appearance. The effect was enhanced by the protrusion of his fangs as his lips were pulled back in a snarl.

I continued to move forward as bullets continued to slam into the building around me. Shoving the butterflies in my stomach down, I vaulted over a bench, and then leapt toward Mr. Brown. I covered most of the twenty feet in a single jump, catching him by surprise. He tried to turn the gun toward me, and I heard the snap of bullets as they flew by me, but his aim was off. I ran two steps, getting inside of the gun, and punched Brown hard across his jaw. His head whipped back, and he actually staggered for a step. The gun fell silent—whether from running out of bullets or just Mr. Brown no longer pulling the trigger, I didn't know—and I grabbed the weapon. The barrel was still hot, and for the second time tonight I felt the palms of my hands burning as I ripped the gun away. I threw the submachine gun as far as I could and heard it clatter and skid along the wooden planks of the pier.

My muscles felt as hard as steel. I had never felt so strong. If you can imagine it, I had been kind of a weakling in the old neighborhood.

Now there's an understatement, Sarah teased.

I got into fights as a kid—who didn't—but I was always on the losing end of them.

And what did I always tell you? Dad asked.

I responded automatically, like repeating some sort of mantra. *You need to fight like a man or they'll always pick on you. Don't ever hesitate or they'll always beat you.*

I took that advice now, throwing multiple punches at Mr. Brown. I saw his face contort under my fists, but in a moment my fists fell on empty air as he jumped out of my reach. He eyed me warily as he worked his jaw back and forth, then dabbed his fingers at a trickle of blood that ran from his nose.

"Heh," he gave a slight chuckle, partly in surprise and partly in admiration. "You been working out with Gene Tunney, Saul?" He narrowed his eyes. "Or maybe you finally stopped being a *lokh* and bled somebody. Who'd you have to kill? Nobody I know, I hope?"

"I didn't kill anybody, but I'm willing to make an exception for you."

Mr. Brown raised one eyebrow at my statement. "You know, Saul, she's going to be really unhappy that she won't be able to complete your transition herself. She was looking forward to it, for some reason."

I tried not to be distracted by what he was saying, but I had to know. "Who? Who are you working for?"

Mr. Brown gave me a coy smile and wagged a finger at me. "And spoil her surprise? I don't think so."

"Fine," I spat. "Keep your little secret. I'll find out soon enough, but you won't be there to enjoy it."

He narrowed his eyes and bared his fangs. "You can try, whelp."

I threw a punch, a large right hook that Mr. Brown ducked back from, a smile of pity starting to form on his face. That's when I kicked him in the balls.

Oy! Why in the world would you do such a thing? Dad asked. *Only* zhlubs *fight dirty, Saul. Be proud and don't stoop to their crude level.*

Dad, you always told me to fight fair. But when you're trying to survive the bullies in the neighborhood, or the goyim *at school—who liked nothing better than to pick on the small Jew-boy—fighting fair takes a back seat to living to see the next day.*

Mr. Brown's face puckered, and his eyes went wide. Then his face contorted with rage and fury, and I swear that his fangs grew at least another inch.

His punch was a blur, and I managed to pull away slightly, but his fist still connected with my jaw. I spun in a circle, and when I came back around, another punch landed on my chest. I flew backwards, my feet actually leaving the ground, and I landed on my back, crushing a bunch of flowers. The bullet wounds that Capone had given me were completely healed, but each of the spots where I had been struck flared with a white-hot pain. Apparently, the wounds were still tender. In addition, there was a sharp pain deep in my chest that told me that Mr. Brown's punch had broken a rib. Maybe two.

I didn't have time to recover, as the leather sole of Mr. Brown's shoe was coming down toward my head. I managed to roll away as his foot smashed into the flowerbed and drove so deep that it smashed through the boards underneath the garden. He pulled his foot free and kicked me, causing me to roll further through a rose bush.

My own blood was rushing through me, pounding in my ears. I managed to stand up and turned to face Mr. Brown. He had also recovered, and we faced each other.

"You may be one of the Gifted now, but you are outmatched. Surrender to me and I'll let your pet live," Mr. Brown waved a hand toward Ness. "Then maybe she'll be able to get you to obey."

I didn't really hear his words, my anger having taken over. I stepped up, hands held at the ready, and threw more punches. A couple of them landed, but Mr. Brown threw his own at me, each of them landing like gunshots.

I ducked my head, lifting my arms for protection as his blows continued to rain down. That's when I noticed the blood seeping from the ragged hole in the leg of his brown slacks; the spot where Ness had shot him. He was probably healed by now, but my own experience just a moment ago was enough encouragement for me. I dropped my left arm and landed a punch hard at the spot where his bullet wound had been. His knee buckled and there was a bellow of pain from Mr. Brown. Then his retaliatory punch landed on the side of my head, and the vision in my right eye instantly blurred. I hit the pier outside of the garden like a sack of potatoes.

I felt two powerful hands grab my head, one on my chin, and the other on my forehead. I knew that Mr. Brown was about to snap my head off the way he'd done with the *jiangshi*.

Chapter 36

Mr. Brown's grip was tightening, and I could feel his muscles clenching. "Won't killing me get you in trouble with your master?" I asked, the words tumbling out quickly. I slipped my hand into my jacket pocket.

"When I tell her how much of a pain in the ass you've become, I think she'll forgive me." His breath was warm across my neck. "Good ridd–"

I didn't let him finish the sentence. I pulled Ness's gun quickly, bringing it up to the side of my head and pulled the trigger. It sounded like a bomb going off inside my ear. I went deaf instantly in that ear and I could feel a trickle of blood running out and down my cheek, but Mr. Brown had released my head. I somersaulted away from him, losing my grip on the gun in the process.

Either my aim had been off—very likely—or Mr. Brown had managed to move out of the way—also very likely—because all I could see was a bright red line across his cheek. The wound was already healing.

My eyes went to the gun laying on the pier and I lunged for it, but he kicked the gun away before I could grab it. He landed a punch to my gut and I went down on my hands and knees. *How the hell can I get the wind knocked out of me if I don't need to breathe?*

His voice was brittle as he said, "Way too much of a pain in the ass."

I saw him pull his leg back, preparing to kick me. As he started to swing the leg forward, I heard the sharp bark of a pistol. His brown overcoat seemed to unravel at a spot just above the elbow and he stumbled to the side, nearly losing his balance, his kick merely tousling my hair.

He yowled a deep, primal cry and spun around just in time for a second bullet to strike his left shoulder. Blood stained his shirt. He looked around the pier and managed to dodge a third bullet. He spat at me and then he turned and ran, dodging around a push cart and running off the pier and toward the boardwalk. Two more bullets chased him, but they smacked harmlessly into the buildings.

I turned to see Christian, his pistol held steadily in his left hand, a bloody bandage wrapped around the wrist. His right arm sat in a makeshift sling. "Took you long enough," I said, managing to sit up. For a moment I thought I was back on the carousel as the pier revolved around me.

"Maybe if I'd not been squeezed like an orange I'd have been here sooner." He turned to look in the direction where Mr. Brown had fled. "Do you think we've seen the last of him?"

I stood up and slowly shook my head. "I doubt it. He's like a bad penny."

Christian turned back and holstered his weapon, then walked over to Ness, who was just now sitting up and holding a hand to his forehead. My own hearing was nearly recovered, just a dull ringing now from the gunshot so close to my ear. The rest of my bruises and abrasions I'd received from my fight now only noticeable as a slight tingling sensation. Even my chest felt normal as I took in a deep breath. I went and picked up Mr. Brown's Tommy Gun and Ness's pistol as Christian helped Ness to his feet.

"Give me one damn good reason why I shouldn't fire the pair of you right now!"

Chapter 37

"I still don't believe that Ness bought it," I told Christian for the hundredth time.

"Saving his life? It was the truth," he shrugged. "But I also don't think he was serious about firing us."

"He sure seemed serious enough to me." I turned to look out of the train's window.

"Besides, he wants to stop Capone just as badly as we do."

"But he wants to do it within the boundaries of the law, and we both know that Capone will never let that happen."

"True. But if he doesn't know about something, he can't stop it."

I turned back to face Christian. "When did you become the rebellious one?"

"Dealing with Capone is God's will, and I cannot rebel against His commands, lest His hand be heavy upon me."

After convincing Ness that we really didn't deserve to be fired, we returned to the hotel to figure out our next move. Ness had given us orders to go back to Chicago while he had to stay here to "clean up our mess". Since we clearly weren't going to do that, Christian and I had instead gone to the President Hotel. There, we learned that Capone and one of his men had already checked out earlier that morning. It only took a little bit of digging, and a few verbal suggestions from me, to learn that they were driving to Philadelphia before catching a train to Chicago.

We caught an express that went straight to Philly, so we'd be in place before Capone reached the city. Short of a direct confrontation, I wasn't sure how we'd be able to take down Capone. He was slippery enough with the law and regular cops. "I'm afraid this may come down to a fight."

"Are you up for it?"

"I'll do what needs to be done." It was a noncommittal answer, but Christian nodded like he knew what I meant.

We pulled into the station in Philly around two o'clock. It didn't take us long to check the schedules and see that the train to Chicago wouldn't leave until nine that night. We found a spot to watch the ticket counter and sat down to wait.

"Do you feel any different?" I asked Christian.

"What do you mean?"

"I mean after I fed on you."

"Besides feeling empty? No. Why?"

"I don't know. I was just thinking about Frank Nitti."

"Why are you thinking about him?" Christian gave me a quizzical glance.

"He works for Capone, but he's not a vampire."

"Well, I'm sure that not everybody in his organization is a vampire."

"But that's just it," I said, staring hard at Christian. "He knows Capone is a vampire. Why would Capone keep him around with that info? And I think Nitti was able to sniff me out at the restaurant."

"Sniff you out? Was he a werewolf?"

I shrugged. "What? I don't know. I don't even know how I'd be able to tell. But he had to have known that I was there and that's why he called Capone."

"And what, you think that you might have some sort of power over me now? Like I'm Renfield to your Dracula?"

"I don't know? I was just wondering."

Christian pointed a finger at me. "Well, stop it. I won't let any monster have command over me. The Lord is my commander."

I nodded and watched the people head about their business at the station. Eventually Christian got up to use the restroom. He returned carrying a newspaper and two paper cups. He handed one of the cups to me with his left hand. I could smell the blood even before he handed it to me. I was overcome by a powerful urge, a need that I'd never felt before when feeding at any other time, came over me. Without thought, my hand reached for the cup, but I managed to stop myself from grabbing it.

"Take it," Christian said, shaking the cup. "We'll probably need you at full strength."

"You know that I have no idea what might happen if I keep feeding on you."

"Who said I would let you? After this you can go back to your cow's blood."

As I took the cup, I saw the edge of a bandage on his right arm as it rested in the sling. I didn't want to guzzle the blood down like a man dying of thirst, so I said, "You didn't want me touching you again?" I nodded at the bandage.

"No. I was afraid that you wouldn't let go this time.

And I'm out of holy water."

I gave him a wry smile and drank the blood. I had another strange thought as Christian's blood flowed down my throat. I laughed softly to myself as I licked out the last drops of blood. "Do you think I'm no longer Jewish after having drunk the blood of a Christian? I mean, you're definitely not kosher."

Christian paused with his own cup—orange juice by the smell—to his lips, shaking his head slowly and rolling his eyes. "Lord, give me patience."

Again, I felt fully alert, fully alive. (Another chuckle to myself.) I hoped that this would be enough to take out Capone.

We spent the rest of the afternoon sharing the newspaper. I was happy to see that the Cubs had won yesterday's game against the Braves, 7 to 4. Kiki Cuyler had managed to hit a home run off of Percy Jones.

Around 6:00pm we saw Capone enter the station with one of his bodyguards. The bodyguard was Frankie Rio, and I knew that he hadn't been at the murder dinner. *Was he a vampire or just a regular member of Capone's gang?*

Capone wore an overcoat, his hands thrust into the pockets. The pair walked across the concourse where Rio appeared to purchase tickets for their trip later tonight. I expected that they'd find a spot to wait in the station, or maybe grab a bite at one of the diners. Instead, they walked back outside. My eyes widened, adrenaline surging into my blood. I tapped Christian on the shoulder and moved toward the exit without waiting to see if he'd follow. *I'm not going to let Capone get away.*

I had to force myself to not run outside or to draw

any attention that might let Capone know that he was being tailed. When I exited the station, I looked around, my eyes scanning the crowd, flicking over all of the commuters. Then I spied Capone's grey fedora in the crowd. Christian had caught up to me, and I pointed toward Capone and Rio.

The two of them waited for the traffic to slow, and then crossed the street. *What are you doing?* I asked myself. *Do you know we're here? Are you leading us into a trap?*

I didn't have any answers. We had to take the risk that Capone might be setting us up.

Chapter 38

We followed Capone and Rio down the street, keeping our distance. "Are they just stretching their legs?" I asked. Christian gave a noncommittal shrug.

Capone and Rio meandered around the sidewalk, laughing at little jokes, and slowing to look at window displays for department stores. Finally, the two gangsters stopped at the Stanley Theater, where they purchased tickets. "What the..." I started to say. The theater was showing *Voice of the City*, a detective flick starring Willard Mack. "Do we wait here?" I asked.

"And risk Capone fleeing out the back entrance?" Christian shook his head, walking toward the theater. We bought our own tickets and went inside. I headed toward the doors, but Christian walked up to the concession stand.

"What are you doing?" I hissed.

He gave me a blank look. "Getting popcorn. I always get popcorn when I watch a movie."

I shook my head. *Who's the professional now?* I wondered.

Like you have room to talk, Dad's voice came through loud and clear.

After purchasing a bag of popcorn, we walked into the theater. It was already dark, the picture just starting, but I was able to make out Capone and Rio sitting about half-way down on the left side of the theater. I took the closest seat, but I was already feeling a subtle tickling on the nape of my neck. *Damn.* Capone would know we were here. I expected that he would get up, and that he and Rio would head toward the exit down by the screen at any moment.

But they didn't. Capone and Rio stayed put and watched the whole picture. Only once did Capone look back toward my seat, and then gave me a wink. When the picture was over, Christian and I kept our seats. Capone and Rio stood up, and I could hear them talking about the movie. Capone had apparently liked it.

As they walked up the aisle, I stood and moved to block their exit. "We're putting an end to you," I reached out to grab Capone, who stood still, glaring at me. Rio moved to block me, and I grabbed his wrist, twisting his arm around his back. He was a big man and tried to resist. Had I been the living Saul, he might have broken my grip, but he couldn't keep the dead Saul from pinning his arm.

"Are you sure you want to do this, Saul?" Capone asked evenly. "Here?" He glanced meaningfully around at the people still exiting the theater.

I looked around. Christian was standing in our row, emphatically shaking his head no. Behind Capone was an old lady, somebody who reminded me of my former neighbor, Mrs. Rabinowitz. Her mouth was open, forming a large "O", and she stared at me as I held Rio's arm behind his back.

I flinched as if struck and released Rio as I took a step back. I felt my face flush.

Dad taunted, *And this is you, not becoming a monster like him? Feh!*

Rio flexed his arm. He let his shoulder hit me as he walked past. Capone stopped next to me, letting the woman go ahead of him with a polite smile. "Everything is fine, ma'am," he purred. She nodded absently and went on her way.

Capone turned back to me. "What you fail to understand, Mr. Imbierowicz, is that I am untouchable." He gave me a thin smile as he put on his fedora. He and Rio walked out of the theater into the lobby.

My blood pounded in my ears and I hurried after the two gangsters. I was tired of Capone and his games. Stepping into the lobby, I stopped suddenly, which caused Christian to bump into me as he walked out of the theater. I needed to do something, to take some kind of action, but the impossibility of what I was seeing rooted me to the spot.

In the middle of the lobby stood Al Capone and Frankie Rio. They were being confronted by two men wearing ill-fitting suits, their wrinkled appearance and loose neckties practically screamed "detective".

One of the detectives held Rio's arm in a grip that I knew Rio could have easily broken free from if he'd wanted. Capone had a hand in his overcoat and the other detective was saying, "Please remove your hand, Mr. Capone. Nice and slow."

Capone complied, pulling out a short-barrel .38 revolver. "What do we have here, Creeden?" asked the detective as he grabbed Capone's arm. My jaw hung open as I watched Capone let him. "Do you have a permit to carry a concealed weapon, Mr. Capone?"

"I'm afraid I don't, Detective." Capone's voice was casual, and I was dumbstruck. Capone could slip by these two local cops as easy as a snake slithered through the grass. But he just stood there, meekly surrendering the weapon. The other detective was pulling another hand-gun from Rio's coat. Rio also made no moves, standing still and following Capone's lead.

"I'm sorry, Mr. Capone, but we'll need to arrest both of you for carrying concealed weapons."

Capone nodded, as if he understood that the two cops were just doing their jobs and didn't mean any dis-respect. This from a man—an undead monster—who'd proudly said that there was no police detective or judge that he couldn't buy. I was still in shock as I watched the two detectives lead Capone and Rio from the lobby. As they neared the doors, Capone turned to look at me. He had a triumphant smile on his face, like he'd just won a huge jackpot. He whispered a single word, so low that I was probably the only one in the lobby that could hear it.

"Untouchable."

Notes and Acknowledgments

As with our first book, *Unremarkable*, we've taken real events and changed them to suit our needs to tell the story. Capone did host a dinner for Alberto (Albert) Anselmi and Giovanni (John) Scalise. Albert and Scalise were gangsters with a growing reputation among Capone's outfit, but they started to work with another gangster and taking side deals, cutting Capone out of income. It didn't take Capone long to find out about their lack of loyalty to him. One of Capone's men, Frank Rio, set up Anselmi and Scalise in a sting to verify their real intentions. With evidence of their disloyalty, Capone holds a banquet to "honor" the men. It is a banquet that neither Anselmi nor Scalise survive. They are found dead in Hammond, Indiana on May 8, 1929. Nobody can confirm if Capone was directly involved in their deaths, but we think that he probably was. (Note: The famous scene in the movie *The Untouchables* of Robert De Niro using a baseball bat on a gangster is supposed to have recreated this banquet and the murder of the two gangsters.)

After this infamous dinner, Al Capone did attend a meeting of other gang leaders from New York, Philadelphia, and Detroit in Atlantic City. The meeting took place between May 12 to 15, 1929, and was part peace conference, with the different gangs agreeing to keep the peace and allow things to cool down in Chicago, as the St. Valentine's Day Massacre had brought a lot of unwanted attention on all of the gangsters. It was also a chance for the gangsters and their political cronies to agree to terms for graft and the like. (It's not called "organized" crime for no reason.)

The events at the end of the book also took place (without the involvement of any vampires as far as we know). After the meeting in Atlantic City, Al Capone and Frank Rio decided to drive home, but their car broke down in Philadelphia. They got train tickets back to Chicago, but the train was later in the night, so the pair decided to take in a movie (*Voice of the City*) at the Stanley Theater. Two Philadelphia detectives happened to spot Capone and, when the movie ended, they stopped the gangster, searched him, and found the concealed weapons. They arrested Capone and Rio, promising that they'd get a slap on the wrist. However, the judge decided to give a harsher punishment and, in less than 24 hours, Capone had been sentenced to a year in prison for carrying a concealed weapon. Some people think the fix was in, that Capone was trying to avoid any repercussions for the St. Valentine's Day Massacre. Others think Capone allowed himself to be arrested to appease the other gang leaders. And others say it was simply a double-cross by the police. Whatever the real reason, we like to think that, in a way, Capone was thumbing his nose at somebody by allowing the arrest to happen.

Coy and Geoff want to thank several people who helped make this book a reality. Jennifer Davis, Tina Rak, Sabra Brown Steinsiek, and Zachry Wheeler all read drafts of the manuscript and gave us useful feedback and made sure our historical references were accurate. Angella Cormier did a fantastic job with taking our vague ideas about the cover and turning them into reality.

About the Authors

The writing duo of Geoff Habiger and Coy Kissee have been life-long friends since high school in Manhattan, Kansas. (Affectionately known as the Little Apple, which was a much better place to grow up than the Big Apple, in our humble opinion.) We love reading, baseball, cats, role-playing games, comics, and board games (not necessarily in that order and sometimes the cats can be very trying). We've spent many hours together over the years (and it's been many years) basically geeking out and talking about our favorite books, authors, and movies, often discussing what we would do differently to fix a story or make a better script. We eventually stopped discussing other peoples work and started developing our own material, first with RPGs and card games, and now we do the same thing with novels.

Coy lives with his wife in Lenexa, Kansas. Geoff lives with his wife and son in Tijeras, New Mexico.